Writing Tall

Published by Merlyn's Pen, Inc.
4 King Street
P.O. Box 1058
East Greenwich, Rhode Island 02818-0964

Printed in the United States of America.

These are works of fiction. All characters and events portrayed in this book are fictional, and any resemblance to real people or incidents is purely coincidental.

Cover design by Alan Greco Design.
Cover illustration by Kathy Szarko. Copyright ©1995.

Library of Congress Cataloging-in-Publication Data

Writing tall : new fables, myths, and tall tales by American teen writers / edited by Kathryn Kulpa.
  p.   cm.
"All of the short stories and essays in this book originally appeared in Merlyn's Pen: The national magazines of student writing"--Acknowledgments.
Summary: A collection of original fables, myths, tall tales, and other tales written by American teens.
  ISBN 1-886427-06-2
  1. Youths' writings, American [1. Literature--Collections.
2. Youths' writings. 3. Fables. 4. Mythology. 5. Tall Tales.]
I. Kulpa, Kathryn.
PZ5.W845   1996
[Fic]--dc20   95-24429
                                                         CIP
                                                          AC

99 98 97 96 95   6 5 4 3 2 1

Writing Tall

NEW FABLES, MYTHS, AND TALL TALES BY AMERICAN TEEN WRITERS

Edited by
Kathryn Kulpa

The American Teen Writer Series
Editor: R. James Stahl

Merlyn's Pen, Inc.
East Greenwich, Rhode Island

Acknowledgments

Jo-Ann Langseth, copy editor, and Christine Lord, managing editor, are gratefully acknowledged for their significant work in preparing these manuscripts for original publication in *Merlyn's Pen: The National Magazines of Student Writing*.

All of the short stories and essays in this book originally appeared in *Merlyn's Pen: The National Magazines of Student Writing*.

The American Teen Writer Series

Young adult literature. What does it mean to you?

Classic titles like *Lord of the Flies* or *Of Mice and Men*—books written by adults, for adult readers, that also are studied extensively in high schools?

Books written for teenagers by adult writers admired by teens—like Gary Paulsen, Norma Klein, Paul Zindel?

Shelves and shelves of popular paperbacks about perfect, untroubled, blemish-free kids?

Titles like *I Was a Teenage Vampire? Lunch Hour of the Living Dead?*

The term "young adult literature" is used to describe a range of exciting literature, but it has never accounted for the stories, poetry, and nonfiction actually written by young adults. African American literature is written by African Americans. Native American stories are penned by Native Americans. The Women's Literature aisle is stocked with books by women. Where are the young adult writers in young adult literature?

Teen authors tell their own stories in *Merlyn's Pen: The National Magazines of Student Writing.* Back in 1985 the magazine began giving young writers a place for their most compelling work. Seeds were planted. Ten years later, the American Teen Writer Series brings us the bountiful, rich fruit of their labors.

Older readers might be tempted to speak of these authors as potential writers, the great talents of tomorrow. We say: Don't. Their talent is alive and present. Their work is here and now.

About the Author Profiles:

The editors of the American Teen Writer Series have decided to reprint the author profiles as they appeared in *Merlyn's Pen* when the authors' works were first published. Our purpose is to reflect the writers' school backgrounds and interests at the time they wrote these stories.

Contents

Be careful what you wish for . . .

Harry's Hurried Childhood

by ALAN MCCABE

I'm real depressed, Doc," Harry Quickman told his psychiatrist. He seemed nervous and on edge, frequently running his sweaty hands through his hair.

"Let us talk, then," replied the psychiatrist, a soft-spoken, calm man who wore a brown suit. The two men sat face to face, the doctor behind a neat and orderly desk, the patient on a cushioned seat. This setup would often become uncomfortable for Harry during the sessions. When those droopy, brown eyes of the psychiatrist began staring into his own, they seemed to be probing his innermost thoughts, boring into his mind and catching everything that was not said. At these times, Harry had to get up and pace about the small, windowless room.

"I'm depressed because I didn't have a childhood," said Harry.

"You told me that before," said the psychiatrist, "but you've never told me exactly what you mean by it." The eyes probed deeper. "You never had a pet, perhaps? You never had any true friends? Your parents were cruel?"

The eyes probed deeper still with each question. Harry stood up and walked back and forth.

"No, Doc, I never had a childhood! Oh, how do I tell you? I've never explained it to you before because I knew you'd think I was crazy. But I gotta tell somebody. Sit back in that chair, Doc; it's a long and bizarre story . . .

"As a kid, I loved Christmas—I absolutely loved it! But for all the childish and selfish reasons: receiving toys and candy, stuffing myself at Christmas Eve dinner, going out to play in the snow, being the center of attention when all the relatives visited. I would look forward to Christmas all year, always wanting everything else to be over and done with so Christmas would come again. My Christmas list was always written by June. As the months went on, I would make so many revisions and additions that by December it would be at least twenty pages long. Every year it was the same. In January I wished there were some way to speed up the year, just so it would be December 25th again.

"One of my favorite Christmas treats was the annual visit from Uncle Titus. He was a peculiar fellow. He traveled extensively and always came back with odd souvenirs from his voyages abroad. Well, on the Christmas which found me at the age of six, Christmas 1949, Uncle Titus presented to me a souvenir which was perhaps the most magnificent of any he'd ever given me. However, because of my selfish eagerness, it turned out to be the most horrible, for it caused me to be deprived of my childhood.

"I remember it all very vividly. I guess that's because it's just about the only childhood memory I can claim. We were all sitting around the tree, the whole family; wrapping paper was strewn about the floor. All my new toys were around me like a mighty fortress. Only a handful of unopened presents remained under the tree.

" 'Where's my present from you, Uncle Titus?' I asked eagerly.

"He took a small wrapped package out of the breast pocket of his plaid pajamas and handed it to me.

" 'It's so little!' I said.

" 'Big things come in small packages,' my infinitely wise uncle remarked.

"I ripped the brown paper wrapping from the parcel; I then had in my hand a small wooden box painted with bright swirling colors—the spiraling design seemed to be turning round and round before my very eyes. A small metal clasp kept the box shut. I unhooked it and looked in the box. I saw nothing.

" 'Uncle Titus, it's empty!' I whined.

" 'Look again, m'boy!'

"I did. And again, I saw nothing. By this I mean absolutely nothing! It was completely black inside that tiny colorful box; looking into it was like looking through a window to outer space. I was about to thrust my whole hand into that box to see if I could pull anything out, but my uncle grabbed my arm, saying, 'No! No! You must let it come to you, Harry!' So I waited quite a while, growing more doubtful by the minute. My mom and dad came to my side. They became as mesmerized as I was by the black void within the box. After many minutes, something began to happen. I could hear a faint whisper, or a hiss—it seemed to be saying something, but quietly and in a foreign language. It grew steadily louder. I then saw a small speck of blue. It was far away in this blackness I was looking into, but it was steadily approaching. Closer and closer this cloud of blue came, getting bigger and bigger. 'Oh my God,' I heard my father, still by my side, whisper.

"Now the blue cloud was at the very edge of the black void, and it swirled around in circles, just like the design on the box. Round and round it went until it began to rise slowly out of the box, heading right for my face! It became thin and bore a resemblance to a fine blue thread. Suddenly, the string of blue smoke darted toward me. I felt a sudden pang of terror as that blue smoke, now more like blue lightning, shot at my face. I opened my mouth to scream—and into my open mouth went the smoke! I felt it go down my throat.

"Trembling, I looked up at Uncle Titus. I could say nothing. Mom and Dad could not speak either. Their faces showed the same fear I felt. Dad finally found his voice and said to his brother (not at all in a voice of approval, either), 'You've really outdone yourself this time, Titus.'

"Uncle Titus patted my head and laughed and said, 'What'd ya think o' that, m'boy? Heh, heh! Now listen close. That was the Blue Smoke of Jooba. I picked it up in Egypt. Make a wish, Harry, and it will come true! Plus (and this is what makes the Blue Smoke of Jooba the finest of all the wishbringers), the smoke is in you now—it's a part of you! It will always be with you. Any time you make that same wish, it'll still come true!'

"Every child's fantasy! Make a wish and it will come true! Well, one and only one thought came automatically to my mind about what my one wish would be. In my selfish little head, I came up with a brilliant plan. Looking at my pile of toys, I pictured it twice as high . . . thrice as high . . . towering up to the sky high! No more would I have to wait for Christmas! I would bring Christmas to me!

" 'I wish it were Christmas 1950!' I said. Everything became pitch black around me, and I felt like I was floating through some kind of thick ooze. I heard the voices of my parents, my friends, even myself—but I could see nothing. I then had the sensation of falling, and I landed lightly on our living room floor. The next thing I knew, there was a whole mess of unopened Christmas presents around me. I quickly got down to business! My greedy little fingers dove into the shiny red wrappings, unraveled the rosy ribbons, bit and tore into the papered parcels, making the sounds I looked forward to all year round: *Ssshhhhk! Ffffft! Rrrrrip!* Soon there was a pile of paper on one side of me and a tower of toys on the other . . . Teddy bears and bright-colored bouncy balls! Candy canes and Candyland! Chocolate Santas and Chinese checkers! Two toy guns and a talking clock! Everything but a partridge in a pear tree. I was in Christmas heaven.

"My family was there, too, of course; it was just like a normal Christmas at the Quickmans'. After opening my presents, I went outside to play in the snow a bit and showed off in front of my aunts and uncles. When the day was over, I wanted Christmas again. I said, 'I wish it were Christmas 1951!'

"I again made that strange journey through darkness and landed in Christmas 1951. And once again, we repeated all our family Christmas traditions—except the one in which we danced around the tree while Bing Crosby sang 'The Little Drummer Boy' on the scratchy record player and then all joined in our 'family hug.' Mom always insisted we do this before we opened any presents, and it drove me insane with anticipation. As we dipped and twirled beneath the tree, I always became dizzy and could not keep my eyes off the enticing collection of gifts. 'Open me! Open me!' they were calling. But all the other Christmas traditions I had no quarrel with: the roast turkey and gravy and mashed potatoes whose delightful aroma filled the house from noon till midnight . . . Aunt Louella telling one of her stories, which were completely pointless and didn't even have a punch line but were great to listen to just the same. All these things I loved. I truly seemed to think they were the only things I loved. And so I skipped over everything else—over and over again, until Christmas 1959—just to get to these moments. Somehow I just did not realize that similar lovely moments occur throughout life, any time of the year.

"I had a huge pile of toys by now indeed, but I suddenly felt unbelievably tired and sad. I was now sixteen years old, and, in my mind, getting toys and playing in the snow did not mean as much to me. Although all the Quickmans were present at each of the Christmases, I had this feeling of missing my family very much. I felt as if I had lost a lot of time that could have been spent with them. And indeed I had! I yearned, for the first time ever, for all the big and little joys that everyday life brings. So I spent all of Christmas 1959, and every day thereafter, with my family. But I was very confused: my family acted as if I had never been gone—as if I had spent the last ten years with them—but I had no memory of it! To me, those ten years had been spent zipping through time and space—nonexistent to me! I had no memory of those years at all! And yet, I had the knowledge and sense of a normal sixteen-year-old.

"So there you have it, Doc. Through a selfish, childish whim, I expunged an entire decade of my existence, perhaps the ten most influential, enjoyable years of a person's life. And I can't get them back. I want to have—or to have had—a childhood!"

"That's a very interesting story," said the psychiatrist.

"But you don't believe it, and you think I'm a loonybird," said Harry.

"Well, it seems to me, Harry, that you have two problems here. You are depressed and you fear that your peers may think you're insane. According to your story, though, one action can solve both problems—wish yourself back to Christmas 1949! The smoke is still with you. You said it granted the same wish every time you wished it—and, by wishing to return to Christmas 1949, you'd be making basically the same wish as you had so many times before: to go to a different Christmas of your life. Make the wish, Mr. Quickman! Go back to Christmas 1949 and change your original wish . . . Find your childhood."

Harry saw he had nothing to lose. If it worked, he would have his childhood back. If nothing happened, he could laugh and say, "I was only kidding. Had you going there, didn't I?"

He closed his eyes and took a deep breath. "I wish it were Christmas 1949!"

"I'll never forget that Christmas!" proclaimed ancient Uncle Titus at the Quickman dinner table on Christmas Eve. "Christmas 1949! It was nearly forty-five years ago, but I remember it as if it were yesterday. When I gave you that Blue Smoke of Jooba, Harry, I thought for sure you'd wish for something silly like a certain toy you had had on your list but didn't receive. Or maybe a million jillion dollars or something selfish like that. But, no, Harry, m'boy, you got philosophical on us, and I'll never forget it! 'I wish to live every moment of my life to the fullest,' you said, 'by enjoying the love of my family and friends.' Took us all by surprise, ya sure did, m'boy!"

It had taken Harry by surprise when he had said it, too. Even now, almost forty-five years later, he had no idea how a six-year-old boy could possibly have thought up such a wish. However, he would never take that wish back—not for all the toys in the world—because he had lived a full, enjoyable life, a life full of pleasant childhood memories.

ABOUT THE AUTHOR

Alan McCabe lives in West Chester, Pennsylvania, where he attends West Chester East High School. "Writing is my main interest," he reports, but he's also an eager collector of Wizard of Oz memorabilia. He enjoys tennis and writing and performing rock 'n' roll songs.

It's, like, grim, you know?

A Modern-Day Fairy Tale

by PAMELA BACHORZ

I was putting on my makeup when Mom called me out to the garden. What a drag. I mean, I can't go out of the house without my blush, bronzer, mascara . . . oh, just everything! I look terrible."

"Oh, yeah, Renee, I know. Mom says it's sooo silly, but, I mean, how else will people recognize me? I've always worn makeup, since fourth grade! Or, maybe third grade . . . gee, who knows how long?"

"Yeah. Anyway, wait, it gets worse. Would you believe? Mom actually wanted me to go visit Gram! In that condition and everything!"

"NO!!"

"Yes! Of course, I said no, but she said 'no new clothes for a month' . . . so what could I do? No way could I survive that. I put on that old winter coat from last year—y'know, the one with that hideous red hood— and walked through the woods because I'd just die if someone saw me . . ."

"The haunted woods? Gosh, I'd rather have someone see me."

"It's not really haunted. Anyway, I was halfway to
Gram's when I saw this kinda dark, skinny thing trying to hide behind trees. Get this, Carla, I swear it was
staring at me! I walked faster and it still followed me."

"What was it? I would've yelled and run!"

"Carla, I had no idea what it was. So, I decided it
was a bird's shadow or something, and I just kept on
going, only I tripped on this dumb root. Geez, can't
trees grow better than that? Anyway, then I got scared
and started to run, and I saw that the shadow was
keeping up with me, but then it disappeared, really
sudden."

"Just all of a sudden, Ree?"

"That's what I said, dip-dip. That it was gone made
me feel better, so I walked slower, because Gram would
worry if I showed up all red and out of breath. I took
my time, and by the time I got to her house it was late.
I was so burned at Mom . . . I mean, I missed my
soaps!"

"That is tough. I'll tell you what happened. You
see, Casey divorced Carlin and Sally married Sophie,
I mean Starla, I mean . . ."

"What?! What was I saying anyway? Oh, yeah. So,
I knocked on Gram's door and she didn't answer. I
knocked again and she yelled real hoarse-like, 'Come
in, dearie.' Kinda weird, if you think about it . . . she
doesn't usually call me dearie. But I went in and she
was in the bedroom, lying in bed 'cause she had a really bad cold. Carla, she looked pretty bad."

"I hope she'll be OK . . . Where else would you get
that extra money?"

"CARLA! Hey, she's my Gram. Don't talk like that. Annnnnywaaaay, she asked me to read the Bible to her, just a few pages. Gad, I hate the thing. It's so darn complicated. I sat in the rocking chair and started to read, but she said her ears were plugged from her cold, and that I should move closer, maybe on the bed."

"Did you?"

"Yep. But after a few sentences, I looked at her and she wasn't listening—just staring at me, and *sniffing*. Her nose must've been pretty stuffed, so I gave her a hankie. Get this, Carla—her fingernails were all uneven and pointy! Not only that, they were sharp! She could hardly hold the Kleenex without tearing it."

"Boy, sounds like a manicure would help. How can people do that? Just let their nails go like that . . ."

"I don't know! So, when I was done, she yawned and I saw her teeth. Carla, they were yellow and pointy! Talk about needing braces and a toothbrush! So, I asked her how they'd gotten like that."

"Ree, no offense, but you probably hurt her feelings."

"Naw, Gram just laughed and said they were to eat me with. I couldn't believe she said that . . . I never thought old Gram had a sense of humor!"

"Why can't *my* grandma be like that?"

"Then, it happened!"

"WHAT?"

"She grabbed me and I saw that she had the biggest eyes and nose! And her arms were so long! She said they were to hug me with—special grandmother arms."

"Hah. They probably were stretched from carrying too many cookbooks, Ree."

"That's what I figured. But, actually, they weren't.

Guess what, Carla?"

"Gee, I don't know. Maybe she's really a gorilla."

"Ha, ha, what a wit. Actually, she's a wolf. Yes, a wolf. She tried to eat me! But Daddy came looking for me and just as she—or maybe he—was going to gobble me up or whatever, he hit the wolf over the head with the Bible! And it was so heavy that the blow to the head killed the wolf! Funny thing is, we can't find Gram."

"Yeah, sure. Tell it to your guidance counselor. Geez, you're really freaked. Call me when you're normal . . . you know, makeup, clothes, boys."

"But I'm telling the truth! Carla? Carla??"

All Renee heard was the buzz of a dial tone. "Why doesn't anybody believe me?" she muttered, flipping through her personal phone directory to find the Grimm brothers' phone number. "Maybe they'll listen . . ."

ABOUT THE AUTHOR

Pamela Bachorz lives in Ballston Spa, New York, where she attends Ballston Spa High School. Her interests include reading, water sports (especially windsurfing), computers, and writing. She wrote this story while a student at Ballston Spa Middle School.

To find a treasure, you must look within your heart.

The Leprechaun's Gold

by CARYN BRADY

Once upon a time there was a poor woodcutter and his family who lived near a deep, dark wood. His three daughters were named Esther, Clara, and Katy. At one time their food supply became very meager, and the faces in the often grieved little household were pale and appeared exhausted. The kind father could not bear to see his daughters starve, so he announced one day, when the last of the bread was nearly gone, "I'm going out to forage for food in the forest today. Perhaps I will find something for us to eat." The women could not protest, so off he went.

It happened that an Irish leprechaun dwelled near the little cabin. The fortunate father seized the little man when he saw him passing. "Aha!" he excitedly exclaimed. "It has been said that when anyone captures a leprechaun, the leprechaun's duty is to share his gold!"

"Hogwash, all of it!" declared the leprechaun, who only reached his captor's knees. He thought awhile and said craftily, "I might give some treasure to one who can prove he needs and deserves it. But how am I to know that you will not spend unwisely and carelessly?"

The woodcutter replied, "I have three young daughters and a loving wife. I should desire only a bit of gold, to provide food for them, so they need not starve!"

"Well!" exclaimed the magic dwarf. "A pitiful story indeed! Very convincing, but how can I trust any human? If you are to prove yourself honorable, caring, honest, and trustworthy, you must be able to make a friend, despite difficult circumstances."

Aha! thought the poor man. *How simple!* He said aloud, "I shall be put to the test."

The leprechaun chuckled with glee. "As you wish!" he chortled. He then pulled out a staff made of polished wood that gleamed like silver. As the staff touched the bewildered woodcutter's shoulder, the larger man suddenly shrank and was transformed into a wretched, ugly dwarf. "To prove you are trustworthy, you may not return home to your family and tell them of your cheerless situation. Instead, on your own, you must befriend someone in three days without informing them of your true identity. That will prove you are caring indeed!" And, with a wink of his green sparkling eye, the leprechaun disappeared.

When near the end of the day the father had still not returned to the cabin, the mother and daughters became frantic. The eldest daughter, Esther, pleaded with her forlorn mother to allow her to go and search for their missing father. At last the anxious woman relented, but warned Esther to return home before dark.

Esther set out into the woods, confident that she

would surely find her beloved father. As the hours passed and stars began to sprinkle the darkening sky, she grew more and more worried. The young girl was about to turn and go back when she happened to see a repulsive dwarf with a crooked nose and a tangled beard. "Ugh!" she shuddered, and began to run swiftly. "Wait!" cried the dwarf. "A man's face does not determine his character!" But the terrified girl ran on.

When she arrived at the cabin, frightened and out of breath, she broke into tears and sobbed out, "I did not find anything but a disgusting old dwarf!"

Upon hearing this, Clara, the second eldest daughter, begged, "Oh, Mother, may I please go search for Father?"

"What makes you believe you can do any better than Esther?"

"I may try, though, can't I?"

"Very well, child. Set out in the morning, and I do wish you all the luck in the world."

As soon as the sun rose, Clara quietly left the house and resolved that she would find her father. She walked on and on until she could walk no farther, and then collapsed from pure fatigue. The dwarf, observing her situation, hastily ran to her aid and helped the maiden to her feet. She turned to thank the little fellow, but one glance at his hideous face and she instantly bolted, despite the dwarf's protests and her weakened condition. She never stopped running until the little house was in sight.

When she walked in the door, Clara, like Esther, began to weep and told them that she too had found only a dwarf. This broke down the courage of them all, except for Katy, who tried to comfort them, though she herself despaired.

"Mother dear, never worry. I shall search for our father."

"Oh, you silly girl!" sobbed her heartbroken mother. "How could you find even a clue of him when your two elder sisters have found only an unsightly troll!?"

But kind Katy pleaded and pleaded, and at last her mother gave in. "You may start off early tomorrow," she said. Katy prayed with all her heart that she might find her father, for she loved him greatly.

As soon as dawn broke, Katy softly closed the door and began to walk briskly through the forest. It grew dark as she passed through a thick, lonely section of the woods, and here she nearly gave up entirely. But something told her to continue, so she asked a white rabbit on her path whether he had seen her father. The tiny animal made no sign that he understood her—but scampered away in a different direction. Katy followed him.

Soon she reached a clearing where the sun's rays shone down brightly. Her gaze fell on a little dwarf with his head in his hands, weeping bitterly. "Oh, do stop," Katy begged. "Whatever is the matter that makes you cry so?"

The dwarf looked up slowly and nearly leaped with joy at seeing his youngest daughter. But he did not show any sign of recognition, as he had promised the leprechaun to tell no one of his true identity. In spite of his frightful appearance, the young girl did not flinch at all.

"I have no friends in the world," explained the dwarf, "because of my ill-looking face."

"I don't mind it a bit," said Katy resolutely, as she

clasped his hands in hers. Then she told him of her troubles.

Just then the leprechaun appeared because it was the end of the third day. He stared incredulously at the dwarf and the maiden, deep in earnest conversation. "Great Saint Patrick!" he exclaimed loudly. "You have actually made a true friend!"

"Yes, he has," volunteered Katy. The dwarf looked up at her appreciatively. The leprechaun once again took out his shimmering staff and touched the dwarf gently on the shoulder, whereupon he immediately sprang back into his original form.

"Father!" cried Katy, as she flew at him with hugs and kisses. They tried to explain very quickly what had happened, both at the same time, and if you have ever been in a similar situation, you'll know they got absolutely nowhere.

The leprechaun was quite generous with his gold and jewels, and Katy and her father thanked him graciously over and over again. Then they returned home, where everyone laughed merrily and kissed and hugged and explained. Because of Katy's kindness, her father's loyalty, and the leprechaun's gold, they all lived happily ever after.

ABOUT THE AUTHOR

Caryn Brady lives in Canandaigua, New York, where she attends Canandaigua Senior Academy. Among her interests are writing short fiction, reading, soccer, canoeing, and sailing.

The town is going to the dogs—but
where are the dogs going?

Dog Days

by LAUREN TERRY

S o you want to hear about the dogs. I remember
them well myself. I was born here, I was raised
here, I've lived all my life here, and at the rate
I've been going lately, I fully expect to die here. The
neighborhood dogs began to act strangely about seven
years ago—yes, seven years to this month. It began
sometime around the beginning of that August.

We all remember that month well, if only for the
heat wave. By August the seventh, we had hit a certified drought, and the temperature reached at least a
hundred and ten degrees every day. Usually, these heat
waves hit in July, but it's not impossible for one to
come so late. In the Deep South, we are always prepared for this kind of thing: throughout our summers,
well-trained air conditioners purr in harmony with the
automatic icemakers in refrigerators. As the summer
began, every yard was a private water park filled with
plastic pools, sprinklers, and those slick yellow slides

that look like rolled-out raincoats. But after around August first, even the children stayed inside. It was too hot to do much more than sweat. The heat was not arid and desert-dry, as it is sometimes, but I wish it had been. No, this heat spoke of heavy, oppressive jungles, where the sun glittered like a gold medallion through the rain, rain that never came to us. We all gave up trying to keep our yards trimmed and watered, so that every street stretched out with crisp deserts of dead grass. The little old ladies (who, by definition, include me, I suppose) despaired over their dying flower beds, but the epidemic of heatstrokes made that problem look like small potatoes.

No one really noticed the dogs for a while, including me. A few people have told me that yes, it began slowly, one dog at a time, and not all at once as I had feared. After all, anything overly conspicuous would have defeated their purpose . . . such as it was. Most people didn't wake up until the situation was irreversible. Each dog chose its own spot in its own front yard—the front steps, the foot of the driveway, in the gutter, beside the mailbox—and never left it, day or night. You could drive down every street in the neighborhood, in your air-conditioned car, and see a faithful, panting dog at almost every house, tail wagging.

At first we blamed the heat. A few people fretted that we might have a pack of mad dogs on our hands— after all, August is the rabies season—but there were no foaming muzzles or glassy eyes, and doesn't a dog have the right to sit in his own front yard? They never bothered anyone, never barked or howled once.

Unless, that is, you bothered them first.

That was another story entirely. Naturally, the owners got worried when their pets wouldn't come in for dinner and wouldn't eat the food they brought. We humans weren't very hungry during all that heat either, but the dogs wouldn't even drink from their bowls. By the laws of nature, they shouldn't have lasted a week, but day after day, the dogs still had bright eyes, toothy grins, and nonstop motors in their tails. They seemed to subsist on fresh air and dew. Moreover, they seemed to be . . . well . . . waiting for something.

God help the poor soul that tried to take matters into his own hands. Drew Kramer down the street, who is thirteen now but was six years old then, tried to drag his golden retriever indoors one day. Sparky would not budge an inch; in fact, he scratched Drew like a cat and nearly bit him. Drew ran inside, almost hysterical, but Sparky was his normal, placid self in an hour. In spite of the heat, I often saw little Drew kneeling by his dog, petting him, and it's that memory that makes me sad when I think of what happened in the end.

Fred Berry next door tried the same stunt as Drew, and managed to haul his Labrador halfway up the driveway until "good ol' Jasper" lost his temper and sank his teeth into Fred. I can still remember Fred screaming bloody murder while he tried to wrestle Jasper with his good arm. No one tried anything after that, especially since the dogs could feel you coming when you were still in the front hall. If you wanted to scratch between Rover's ears for old times' sake, fine, but if you had dangerous ideas in your head, well, they weren't having any of that. It was almost comical to see Sheila Brachman, my other next-door neighbor, shying away from her Buffy. You wouldn't think that a toy poodle could put up much of a fight, but something had gotten into these dogs, and it wasn't just the heat.

This lasted more than a month. No one called the police or the local news; no one talked about it much at all. It was just downright strange, and a thing like that's best left to itself. Then the drought came to an end in, let me see, early September. Yes, I remember, it was the sixth of September. It didn't just rain that night, as I recall; it stormed fit to flood the city. Such a storm as I have never seen before or since—the thunder roared until the streets shook. And the lightning! It came in every color of the rainbow—streaks of scarlet and blue, yellow and violet, emerald and orange, from clouds with dark-veined fingers arching greedily over the streets. And it was lightning, no matter what supernatural hocus-pocus anyone else tells you, because I watched it zigzag from the clouds myself. Apparently, the Fourth of July was being celebrated a month or two late up in heaven.

We forgot the dogs that night; we were too scared for our own skins. To hear Fred Berry tell the story, you would think that we were all scheduled to meet our Maker that night. But then again, I can't really blame him. His house had been struck by lightning once before, and between "lightning never strikes twice" and "man's best friend," I guess it's hard to have faith in much of anything.

The reason everyone couples the storm with the dogs is because of what we found the next morning. Or rather, what we didn't find. We had the normal storm damage—only doubled: fallen branches, flooded gutters, loose roof shingles, trees scarred by lightning, the occasional broken window, and the like. But every single dog was gone. I'm positive they didn't leave merely to seek shelter, for no one has seen hide nor hair of those dogs since. I believe that the storm, or whatever might have come with it, was what the dogs were waiting for. But here's the thing: one dog's paw prints could have been lost in the rain, but forty or fifty is a veritable stampede. Evidence of a mass exodus should have still been there after even a few hours, but not a trace could be found. We have no idea of where they went or exactly when they left. The only clues remaining were the dents where the dogs' haunches had been for the last month.

The dogs left a lot of broken hearts behind, especially the neighborhood children's. Dogs have a habit of wagging their way into people's hearts; I've never known another animal so willing to worship its master. It wasn't as painful as it could have been, though. I think the dog owners had already been mourning for a month. As Sheila, Buffy's survivor, put it, "She weren't my dog no more."

Still, it was hard, considering that several people had more than one dog; some of these animals were older than their kids. A few "missing" posters were plastered on the outskirts of town, and a few search parties scattered out, as if it would do any good. The dogcatcher was even interrogated, but the sane light of reason argued: Him? Take all those dogs? In that storm?

So life went on. People bought or adopted new dogs, although I doubt they ever forgave and I'm sure they never forgot. To this day I'm thankful that my cat was spared. No one knows why it all happened, but a few people have mentioned the old Pied Piper story.

Somehow, I doubt that the Pied Purebred is lurking behind kennels and dog pounds, but at least it was the dogs and not the children.

That was then, and this is now. We've had seven years without a ripple of disturbance. They say that things come in seven-year cycles, and it's August again. I doubt my heart was the only one that stopped beating for a moment last week when I went out to get the morning paper. Tails thumped rhythmically on grass and pavement as blank, happy eyes met mine, and I knew that it hadn't ended with that storm seven years ago. I knew that it might never end. If only we knew why . . .

The dog days are here again.

ABOUT THE AUTHOR

Lauren Terry wrote this story while a student at Homewood High School, in her hometown of Homewood, Alabama. In the Seventeen *1993 Fiction Contest, she won Honorable Mention for a story she submitted. She plans to take creative writing courses. Other hobbies include sketching and softball.*

You be the jury!

Goldilocks vs.
the Three Bears

by DANIEL PALUMBO

Ladies and gentlemen of the court:
 For the past few centuries you have heard
only one side in the case of Goldilocks and the
Three Bears. You all know the lie you were told in
which gentle and loving Goldilocks sneaks into the
mean bears' home and accidentally makes a few good-
natured blunders. I, however, will tell you the story as
it truly occurred.

What happened was that my dear wife, Mama Bear,
made some delicious salmon eye porridge. Upon tast-
ing it we all—I, my wife, and Baby Bear—found it to
be much too hot and decided to take a late-night stroll.
Since our neighborhood was quite safe, I felt secure
leaving the door open and the porridge on the table.
Unfortunately, I was not aware that Goldilocks, on pa-
role from a nearby detention center, was free to wreak
havoc upon our world.

After we left, she carefully sneaked into our home

and began to pillage. First she tried our chairs. She found mine to be too high, so she cut off the legs with a saw. She then sampled my wife's chair, found it too low, and carved obscene pictures on it. My son's she found just right, so she sat on it and broke it.

She then moved on to our porridge. Mine was too hot, so she spit in it; my wife's too cold, so she spilled it all over our good rugs; and my son's just right, so she ate it.

After that she went upstairs to test our beds. She decided mine was much too hard, and so, with no remorse, she hacked it to bits with an ax. Then she moved on to my wife's bed and, finding it too soft, poured honey all over it. However, she liked my son's and fell asleep there, tired from her exertions.

Upon returning, we found destruction everywhere. We cautiously followed the tracks of porridge to Baby Bear's bedroom. There we found her sleeping, oblivious to the world. Suddenly she awoke, screamed, and fled with an assortment of jewels and odds and ends.

As a result of our loss of wealth and my son's resulting psychiatric disorder (requiring extensive medical attention), I am suing the defendant, Ms. Goldilocks, for $3.8 million.

I hereby conclude my statement.

Respectfully submitted,

Papa Bear

ABOUT THE AUTHOR

Daniel Palumbo lives in Bayonne, New Jersey. He wrote this story as a student at the Vroom Learning Center, also in Bayonne.

An old woman's strange tale . . .
and a surprising discovery.

The Curse of Savoll

by HEATHER FITZGERALD

The morning sun rises high above the sleeping village of Savoll, sweeping away the grayness of night. Birds chatter blissfully in the forest and swoop through the hazy sky. Grassy meadows are fresh with dew, and wildflowers raise their faces upward. The terror of night is forgotten.

In the village center, a bell rings from the clock tower. Its voice sings throughout the valley that all is well, and house doors are warily unbolted. The village people peer out into the peaceful morning, relieved to see the splendid sun and ready to work through the warm day. Too soon the bell will toll again and call them home.

On this summer morning, the men of Savoll find fences broken and animals scattered. Their fields are trampled and orchards picked of fruit, yet they are still lighthearted. Glancing at the sun, they smile and laugh as they go about their tiresome chores.

"It is good to be alive!" they tell each other.

In their cottages, the women hum joyfully as they send their children to pick berries and chop wood for their cooking. They open their windows, letting sunshine stream into their homes.

"What a lovely day!" they call to each other.

The village children laugh all morning as they help their parents make bread and mend fences. Sometimes, when work is done, they go to the lake to swim or they play hide and seek in the forest. Not today, though . . . Today they will visit Oma.

"Hurry, Ivry! Oma will tell the story without us!" Thomas called from ahead.

"I am, Tom! I am. These buckets are heavy."

Thomas appeared from behind a huge evergreen and took the buckets. Through the trees they ran, across a stream and through the meadow. They stopped when they reached a tiny cottage resting behind a slender clump of pines.

"*Shhhhh*," said Thomas, dropping the buckets and taking Ivry's hand.

Inside the house, the two joined with other village children around a bewitching old woman they called Oma. Her eyes were alert and dancing, though her face was wrinkled and her limbs gnarled with age.

Tangled silver hair cascaded around her shrunken body as she sat knitting in an old rocking chair. Her voice was cracked and dry, but her stories were exciting and the children would sometimes sit for hours just listening to the many tales she could spin. "Tell us of Millicent," said one child. "Yes, yes . . . please!" the others pleaded.

The old woman's eyes grew narrow, and she hunched over, her face moving closer to the children's as if she were about to confide a dark secret.

"Once . . . a very long time ago," she began, her voice almost a whisper, "an evil witch lived in the mountains above Savoll. Each night she would come down into the village and steal the village people's animals and their food. She became so terrible that the people sought a magician from the East to cast her into darkness. For many weeks he worked, secretly creating a spell that would banish the evil witch from Savoll . . . forever."

Oma stopped suddenly and glared into the wide eyes of each child.

"On the night before the magician's spell was to be completed, the witch, disguised as a traveler, overheard the villagers' plan. Fleeing to her castle, she could find nothing in her books of black art to stop the magician's spell, but she did find a way for the villagers to be punished. A wall of thorns, hundreds of feet higher than the largest pine, would grow around the village of Savoll that night. Never again could the people leave . . . they were doomed to spend generation after generation trapped in their forest valley, hidden from the world.

"The evil witch's revenge was not completed, though. From her ring she took a blood-red stone and placed it in her cauldron. Through the remaining hours of night she worked, casting spells and mixing potions. All her powers of darkness were being set within the stone.

"When the sun had climbed high over the mountains, the witch replaced the stone in her ring and went to the lowest chambers of her castle. There she kept her only daughter—Millicent, a hideous bloodthirsty creature that slept by day and roamed the dungeons by night. Only the witch's magic kept her from escaping, for Millicent would destroy everything within her grasp. The evil witch placed the ring on Millicent's right hand.

" 'She will learn to use my witchery one day,' she reassured herself.

"At noon the next day, the magician's spell was cast upon the witch's castle. A wail of agony rose from deep within; then the forest became silent. And from that moment on, the witch was never to be heard from again. The villagers destroyed her castle in a bonfire that blazed into the night, and her books were burned. Because of the excitement, though, a hideous beast was not noticed as it slipped into the forest.

"Before dawn, after much celebration, the magician left Savoll only to discover a gigantic wall of thorns had grown over the road. When he realized the witch had cursed the village, he hurried back toward Savoll to warn the people and break her spell. But before he could reach the village, wicked laughter broke from out of the darkness, freezing him to the narrow dirt road. An enormous creature jumped from the bushes and slashed the magician with its long, cruel sword. He was found by the villagers the next morning, his bleeding and twisted body thrown before the clock tower. From that time forth, the people of Savoll have lived in terror of night . . . terror of the darkness between dusk and dawn.

"Millicent still roams the countryside, stealing animals and killing all those caught out after dusk."

Oma's voice faded and the room was thick with silence as her mind turned to other thoughts.

"Millicent murdered my own husband many lonely nights ago . . . He was trying to escape through the wall of thorns."

The children sat staring into her expressionless eyes, remembering their own terror as they heard dogs barking and saw Millicent's shadow cast before their cottages.

"Will she ever go away?" a tiny child with auburn hair asked.

"Only if she is challenged . . . only if the ring is pulled from her finger and thrown into the bottomless depths of the lake. Many have tried, children . . . many have died. Ha, ha, ha, ha!" Oma's voice cackled through the room, startling the children. "Go, my dears! Finish the work your parents asked of you, then be home . . . before Millicent finds you! Ha, ha."

The children ran from the house, and Oma sat chuckling and knitting . . . thinking up grand tales.

"She frightens me!" Ivry said as they came upon a boysenberry patch beside the lake.

"She's just old," Thomas told her.

The afternoon wore on while Thomas and Ivry caught fish and played in the sun. Their berry buckets were filled to overflowing, and the crystal waters of the lake invited them for a swim.

"What a delightful place," Ivry said as she finished her swim and lay down under a tall pine. When Thomas went to sit beside her, she was sound asleep. He sat against the tree thinking of Millicent, until he, too, drifted off in dreams . . .

Dong . . . dong . . . The bell in the clock tower began to toll, awakening Thomas and Ivry with a start. The afternoon had faded away, leaving them in the darkness of night. They lay still, too terrified to move.

"It's *dark*! Millicent always finds those caught in the forest after dark!" Ivry whispered to Thomas, choking back tears.

"We have to get home! Quick!" Thomas said, taking her hand and pulling her from under the tree.

They ran through the black forest, bumping trees and stumbling over vines. Moonlit shadows jumped at them—each one an imaginary Millicent with sword in hand.

"Tom! I'm so tired!" Ivry sprawled over a tree stump and fell to her knees. Thomas ran back and pulled her under the sheltering boughs of a pine to rest. Just then, from the corner of his eye, Thomas glimpsed a towering shadow that moved stealthily between the trees.

"Millicent!" he whispered harshly to Ivry, pulling her farther beneath the limbs.

"Children," a voice rasped. The shadow stopped by the tree where they huddled. "I know you are here."

There was a sudden splitting as Millicent's sword slashed deep into the pine, but Thomas and Ivry had already darted from beneath its murderous blade. Dodging trees, they seemed to fly, but Millicent pounded behind them . . . each step bringing her deadly sword closer.

They broke from the forest and into a meadow, Millicent's hot breath upon their necks as she laughed wickedly. Raising the sword above her head, she brought

it crashing down between them. "Help us!" Ivry
screamed into the night.

Millicent raised her sword again and the chase continued, the darkness and the children's cries hiding the
rushing river ahead. As Millicent's sword descended
for a third strike, the children reached the river and
splashed into its frigid waters. Millicent followed, but
her relentless blade pitched between two jagged stones,
and she stumbled headfirst into deep water. As Thomas
and Ivry managed to reach tree branches overhanging
the river, they watched Millicent clutching wildly at
vines and delicate grasses, trying to save herself. But
she was soon swept to the middle of the river and disappeared downstream.

"She's gone, Thomas!" Ivry called above the rushing water.

With Ivry clinging to his back, Thomas pulled them
through the tree branches and out of the water. They
lay on the sandy embankment, gasping for breath from
their narrow escape. Regaining their strength, Thomas
and Ivry listened, motionless, to the powerful water.
As the moments flew by, the river's torrents became
almost deafening to their ears, but the rushing water
could not drown out the sudden peal of laughter that
froze the children's blood.

"I see you lying there! You can't hide!" Millicent
was taunting them from the opposite bank. The moon-
light showed her silhouette as it disappeared into the
shadows.

"We can't escape, Tom! I can't run another step,"
sobbed Ivry.

"Hush! Stay near me!" Thomas ordered. "If she
finds a spot to cross the river, she'll hide and wait for

us in the darkness." Thomas guided Ivry back to the
water's edge. He had seen something else outlined by
the moon's light, something that gleamed wickedly.

Cautiously, Thomas and Ivry inched their way into
the shallows of the river, their eyes searching for Millicent
in the thick trees surrounding them. Finally they reached
the stones that secured Millicent's sword. They grasped
it timidly. Pulling at the leather handle, they found
that its blade was firmly embedded between the rocks.
They grasped the weapon tighter and pulled with all
their might, but the sword would not budge. A cloud
drifted slowly over the moon, dimming its light, as
Thomas and Ivry made one final effort.

"It's hopeless!" Ivry whispered in despair.

Without warning, there was a sudden rustle from
within the trees. Ivry began to scream hysterically as
Millicent burst from the undergrowth. Her laughter
rose above the river's voice, and her clawed fingers
were outstretched, ready to tear into the children. Thomas
leapt upon the rocks and violently jerked at the wedged
sword. Just as Millicent's arms wrapped around his
body, he wrenched it free and secured it against his
chest. With one muscular hand, Millicent lifted him
skyward, preparing to dash him against the jagged
rocks at her feet. Thomas's thoughts whirled and time
seemed to pause until, at last, he gathered enough
strength to raise the sword. He swung its stout blade
against her upraised arm and felt it slip from his bruised
and bleeding fingers. Millicent cried out in horror as
they both toppled to the riverbank. She writhed and
tossed over the sand, shrieking in agony. But suddenly,
with one swift surge, she was back on her feet—the
children forgotten. Millicent fled back into the forest,

cradling all that remained of her right arm. Her horrible wails echoed through the children's minds as they raced, hand in hand, back to Savoll.

Glorious morning came, and the men of Savoll tramped somberly to the riverbank, led by Thomas. A broadsword of fine bronze rested in the river's shallows, and a ring containing one blood-red stone lay in the sand. A large procession of villagers carried these items to the tranquil waters of the Bottomless Lake and flung them into its center. The waters began to steam and boil with heat until Millicent's evils disappeared far beneath the surface. When the lake had calmed, the villagers shouted in jubilation. The witch's curse was broken! Her wall of thorns dried and crumbled in the morning sun, and Millicent never again rampaged through the night.

All was well in Savoll and life rolled by with a peaceful hum. The men and women worked and laughed, rejoicing that they were alive, and the children helped their parents and swam in the lake. Sometimes they would visit Oma who still sat in her old rocking chair, the shawl she had always been knitting wrapped tightly around her huddled body. She spun exciting tales and never failed to tell the story of Millicent and how young Thomas and Ivry escaped her terrible sword. Life in Savoll was undisturbed and joyous forever after.

It was many years later, as Oma's ancient body was being prepared for burial, that the villagers of Savoll discovered that her right arm was missing.

ABOUT THE AUTHOR

Heather Fitzgerald lives in Murray, Vermont, where she is a student at Murray High School. She says that her "very most favorite thing is . . . everything! You can try everything worthwhile at least once, except asparagus." Among her interests are tennis, aerobics, and "learning . . . I love to learn."

The "trial of the century" in ancient Greece . . .

In Defense of Hades

by SARAH-SCOTT BRETT

Your Honor, ladies and gentlemen of the jury, honored guests, the plaintiff would lead you to believe that my client, Hades, is a cruel, evil god, who stole a young woman from her innocent existence and caused much trauma. Such is the nasty, untruthful picture painted by the overprotective mother of a bored young goddess. From extensive research, thorough investigation, and in-depth interviews with innumerable gods, humans, and other assorted beings, I have discovered the truth.

Let me begin at the beginning. After the Titanic Wars led by Zeus and his two brothers, there was much organizing to do. The brothers (Zeus, Poseidon, and Hades) decided to draw lots to decide who got what realm. You see, ladies and gentlemen, none of them wanted the underworld! None of them. So, when it was over and Hades was stuck with it, there was no possibility of compromise. As a matter of fact, Hades begged, literally begged Zeus to allow him to change to a nomadic reign, one that would allow him to roam and be the god of travelers, and to give the underworld to one of his yet-to-be-born sons. But Zeus, the ruler of all, decided that he would rather exile his brother than one of his own sons.

Now, I want to stop here a minute to make an important point: Up until that time, Hades was a young, kind god who loved the sun more than Persephone ever has or ever will. Yet he was deprived of his greatest love and sent to live under the purple sun of Tartarus. How would that affect you? Hades was turned into a hardened god, yet inside he still grieves for the great loss he suffered because of his brother Zeus's pride.

Zeus, in response to his brother's pleading, unfeelingly said, "Be content. Though now you have no people in your kingdom, in time it shall be well peopled. All who live shall in the end come your way. You have, moreover, in your keeping, all the vast wealth that lies hidden in the earth. You shall be the god of wealth; you shall be Pluto, the wealthy one!" (Herzberg, Max. *Myths and their Meaning*. Allyn and Bacon, Inc., pp. 152-153). Be content. Easy for the lord of the universe to say.

Imagine Hades's delight when he sees a young maiden sitting under a tree, trying to keep dry in a thunderstorm. His hard heart melts as he hears her wishing for a place where it never rains, never hails, and essentially is the perfect paradise. And he knows just the place for her—the Elysian Fields! This is where the blest go, those who have never sinned. "Here fell not hail or rain or any snow nor ever winds blew loudly" (Herzberg, p. 182).

Cautiously stepping closer, careful not to reveal his presence, he finds that it is Persephone, the daughter of his sister, Demeter. At first he thinks he ought not go to her because Demeter, whether she admits it or not, has a terrible temper. But poor Persephone looks so bored and wet and unhappy. So Hades approaches and says hello and tells her who he is and what he's thinking. At first she is a bit frightened, backing off and feeling wary. But then she stops and thinks, Why not? I'm not going to get an opportunity like this again, and I'm not going to be ruler or queen of anything else, so why not? Now, we're used to the child inheriting his parents' things, whether it's money, land, or realm, but these are immortals. Her mother will not die. We're not talking about the daughter of a queen who will someday be a queen, in either the same or a different kingdom. This child will not get anything because she won't inherit anything. She won't be given anything by Zeus and the other gods because she was born last. There's nothing left!

Hades and Persephone talk for a long while, and in the end they decide that Hades should talk to Zeus about it. Hades tries to talk Persephone into talking with her mother, too, but no, Demeter would never understand; she thinks her daughter should be happy the way she is, a girl eternally caught between childhood and adulthood. And who wouldn't be happy as the adored baby of Mt. Olympus? She gets to roam the planet, playing in field, forest, stream, and ocean, making daisy chains, flower-crowns, and other such things. If they did go to Demeter she would probably say that Hades had talked her into it, that it was just a phase that she would grow out of. Then she would proceed to lock Persephone up in their palace for a long while until she was satisfied there would be no more talk of her dear brother. Agreeing that it would be futile, Hades and Persephone decide to meet again in two weeks.

Meanwhile, Hades goes to Zeus, saying that he wishes to marry Persephone, and who happens to be outside the door, eavesdropping, but Demeter! She thinks that this is some plot to make her beautiful Persephone as cold as he seems to be. This makes her so scared and so furious that she bursts into the room and screams that if Zeus allows this she will personally make known to Hera all fifteen of his last flings. What can the poor god say? Zeus tells Demeter to calm down, that maybe Persephone and Hades had actually fallen in love. Demeter then shrieks that if they had been together, which she was certain they hadn't, she would make sure they never were again. And with that, she stalks out.

Two weeks pass and Hades meets a crushed Persephone, whose mother had come home raving about the nerve of Hades and warning her daughter to avoid him at all times. Hades, while listing the possibilities, mentions that they could elope. Persephone jumps up from the rock on which she has been sitting and throws her arms around his neck, saying that they would deal with her mother after they were married. A scene then takes place that could have come straight from a movie. The two climb into Hades's chariot and go riding off into the sunset until the earth opens and swallows them in.

Upon their arrival at the gate to Hades, Hades announces that they will be going on a grand tour. Furthermore, he states that he refuses to be called Hades any longer, that from now on he wants to be called by one of his other names, either Pluto or Dis. Persephone decides on Pluto, then insists on him calling her Core, the pet name given to her by Zeus and her mother. They ride down the long passageway laughing, a sound rarely heard either in that hall or from Pluto's lips.

As they reach the Styx, the first of the five rivers which mark the boundaries of Hades, they hear Cerberus barking. Persephone is frightened of the large, three-headed dog with a dragon's tail, but Pluto just laughs and says that he has given Ares the right to pet him, feed him, and throw stars for him to fetch and so Persephone should not be afraid.

Charon, the miserly old ferryman who takes dead folk across the Styx, grumbles when he sees the new queen because he knows it's just going to mean more free rides across for gods and goddesses, which will cut down on the number of people he gets across, thereby lowering the amount of oboli he gets. Pluto and Persephone ride across and Persephone comments on the dreadful color and odor of the river. Now she understands why an oath taken on this river by a god is never broken.

They pass the other four rivers: Lethe, the River of Forgetfulness; Acheron, the River of Woe; Phlegethon, the river that flows fire instead of water; and Cocytus, the River of Wailing. Persephone is beginning to have her doubts about living in this place for eternity, but she keeps silent, hoping that Pluto will show her something that will make it worthwhile. Pluto turns to her and tells her to close her eyes because they are approaching the palace. He leads her to the middle of its courtyard and tells her to open her eyes. She looks around and tries not to look too dismayed, but Pluto can sense something anyway. It's a dark, gloomy place surrounded by foreboding dark trees; close by stretch meadows of asphodel, the lily of the dead. Persephone turns to him and says, "Are these the flowers you were speaking of?" Quickly Pluto answers, "No, of course not. Those are in Elysium; you'll see them later. Now let me show you to your room."

They walk to a beautiful suite where Persephone can see three women standing behind a curtain. Pluto announces that he has three servants to wait upon her. They step out from behind the curtain and Persephone gasps in horror. They are winged maidens with serpents twined in their hair and blood dripping from their eyes. Pluto sees her response and says that if she doesn't want them, they can go back to what they did before she came: pursuing those who escape punishment for the crimes they committed and bothering them with all the horrors of a guilty conscience. Persephone quietly says that she would rather have her attendant from the surface, so Pluto dismisses the trio and goes to search for three gentleladies willing to wait on his queen.

Persephone looks out only one window, having express orders not to look out the others. She sees people standing around, listless and blank. "That is the Field of Asphodel," she hears a voice say from behind her. She spins around and finds herself facing a mysterious Titaness. "I am Hecate, the goddess of witchcraft and sorcery. I managed to retain power after Zeus fought against Cronus. I send ghosts up to haunt the living. You were looking at the place where people are sent to wait for nothing, after they are judged, if they are found to be neither good nor bad. They are just dead. I expect I will be seeing more of you." And on that cheery note, she disappears.

Just then, Hades returns with the earthside attendants. "Here they are, queens all three, I think. You'll be waited on royally. Now let's go see the paradise I promised you."

They walk out through the suite to a small courtyard. Surprisingly, it is bright and flowers are growing, and there is a fountain in the middle spouting clear water. Persephone starts to say how much she loves it, but Pluto cuts her off: "You think this is all? Go through the gate."

She does, and finds everything he had described to her—orchards of beautiful fruit, sports, dancing, singing—an endless bliss, just as he had promised her! Even warriors are resting, "their armor rusting, their chariots unused" (Herzberg, p. 182).

Endlessly she played here, dancing and singing along with the others, feasting and napping beneath the purple sun and shining stars. The only time she was torn away from this was when Hades requested her presence at a judgment or some other gathering. She sat upon her throne next to him, sometimes playing with the keys to the underworld or Pluto's magic staff, other times examining the writing on his trident or making crowns out of cypress branches. A few times she asked if she, too, could wear his cap of darkness, but the answer was always no. She wished she could be outside playing with the new friends she had made.

It was at one of these judgment sessions that Hermes found her. He came down and saw her bored; it seemed to him that she must always be so! Hermes demanded that in the name of Zeus, she be returned to her mother. The gardener overheard this, and, as just that day he had seen her eating out of a pomegranate, he leapt in and shrieked, "She has eaten at least six seeds. The law of the underworld is that she must stay."

By this time Persephone was crying because she would have to leave her happy life and go back to the boring existence she had led, doing the same things every day and avoiding mortals. Hermes took this as a sign that she was afraid she would have to stay and was troubled, for he knew that she must remain if they were to uphold the laws.

Persephone prepared to visit her mother and tell her the truth. But when she and Hades actually arrived, Demeter ran out, grabbed her, and pulled her away; then she started screaming at Hades! What could poor Persephone do? To tell the truth now would be like exiling herself from her mother, which she didn't want to do.

So now the judgment is up to you. We know from the story of Orpheus and Eurydice, how Orpheus convinced Pluto to let Eurydice go; it should be clear to us now that Pluto is not there to punish the dead. Said Museus, "Or bid the sound of Orpheus sing/Such notes as warbled to the string/Drew iron tears down Pluto's cheek/And made Hell grant what love did seek" (Herzberg, p. 187).

My client is not so cruel as to take a mother from her daughter, or, in this case, a daughter from her mother. All we ask is that, for each of the six seeds that the gardener saw Persephone eat, one month in Hades be granted her. The other six months may be spent with her mother. Thus will the laws above and the laws below be equally upheld, and the causes of both justice and love served.

ABOUT THE AUTHOR

Sarah-Scott Brett lives in Durham, North Carolina, and attends Riverside High School. A lover of "anything involving water," she takes special pleasure in stream-walking in the mountains. Computer role-playing, reading, and acting are also important to her. She hopes to one day study drama in England.

An orphaned boy finds friendship—and courage.

The Boy and
the Elephant

by GRANT RIPPETOE

Deep in the vast jungles of India slept the young
Marathi, the last descendant of the courageous
and once-powerful family, the Gondas. His sleep
was interrupted by a mighty roar that echoed throughout the jungle. He put his cherished knife from Grandfather's past in its sheath, wrapped up his also-cher-
ished net, and began searching for the direction of the
ferocious cry. The jungle can be a very confusing en-
vironment. The sounds that come from within rever-
berate all around. Birds chirp and caw from above,
and the noise from monkeys echoes wildly from everywhere. Marathi concentrated deeply and turned to the
left and then abruptly to the right, dashing through
the trees and thick plant life. He made his way toward
the river.

He was coming closer to the deafening noise when
he saw a most amazing sight: a giant elephant almost
twenty feet high. It was trapped in a pit and was stomp-

ing around furiously. The elephant was magnificent.
It had golden tusks, a tail that resembled a whip, and
ears as big as sails. The elephant had an aura of great-
ness. Marathi stood spellbound, watching in bewil-
derment this mammoth beast. The elephant again gave
out a screeching roar. The earth trembled and Marathi
fell to his knees. He spoke to the elephant in a most
tender voice. "You are a mighty creature. Never have
I seen an animal as great as you." The elephant stopped
pacing and rolled his eyes to the edge of the pit where
Marathi knelt. Again he spoke to the beast calmly. "My
ancestors have told stories about an animal such as
you. But I am amazed to actually see you. I don't know
if I should believe my eyes. Perhaps I'm dreaming!"

Slowly the giant elephant raised its head in a regal
manner and looked directly into Marathi's eyes. Marathi
then realized the power and true strength of this beast
as the elephant's eyes squinted and studied the details
of the boy's face. For the first time Marathi felt afraid.
"You are not dreaming," said the elephant, "and if you
call this a dream, I scoff at you, because I would surely
call this a nightmare!"

Marathi's eyes widened in disbelief that an elephant
could talk. Again the beast spoke. "You are frightened,
yet you have nothing to fear from me. Did not your
ancestors tell you I could speak?"

Marathi remained frozen, unable to reply, but managed to shake his head from side to side. The elephant
said, "Very few humans know of my speaking ability.
Help me out of this pit, boy, descendant of wise, courageous, and truthful storytellers."

Marathi was willing to do what he could for the
elephant. He threw his net down into the pit, and it

draped over the beast. The elephant circled until it was wrapped around him. Marathi then cut down some giant vines and tied them to the net.

"Good," said the elephant, "I will call my brothers to assist." He roared loudly, sending a trumpet-like sound through the jungle.

There was a tremendous trembling on the jungle floor, and a herd of elephants soon came charging through the thick trees. They each took hold of a vine and heaved with all their strength. The mystical elephant was lifted up and rolled over onto the ground. He shook off the dust and stood towering over the other elephants. They hailed him with roars, and he bellowed in return.

The huge elephant turned to Marathi and said, "You are brave, young one, and wise for your age. I thank you, but now I must go."

"Where will you go, elephant? Let me come with you."

The elephant chuckled and shook his head. The boy pleaded with the elephant, but the elephant just said, "Go home, boy. Go home to your mother."

The boy replied, "I have no mother."

The elephant then said, "Well, go home to your father, or uncle, or grandfather."

Marathi hung his head and said, "I have no family. I have no one."

The elephant looked intently at Marathi. "Come closer to me, boy. You can stay with me tonight. Now put your foot on my trunk, and I will lift you to my back."

Marathi stepped forward onto the elephant's trunk and was lifted up in the most regal manner. He felt so secure and honored to be sitting on the back of such a magnificent animal. The elephant then proceeded to journey through the jungle brush.

"What is your name, young one?" asked the elephant.

"I am called Marathi. Do you have a name, elephant?"

"Yes, my name is Hartha. You must be very brave and wise to survive in this harsh land by yourself, Marathi," said the elephant.

"Yes," replied Marathi, "but I am also sometimes lonely. And there are times when I do get scared, and also times when I am not so wise."

The beast quietly chuckled and said, "You are still young and have much to learn."

"Maybe you could teach me, Hartha. I have heard stories of your wisdom."

Hartha answered, "I have a dangerous journey to embark upon."

"Do you think it's possible that I could make this journey with you?" inquired Marathi.

"My quest will take me over many lands, and I will face demanding challenges, but the reward if I am successful will be great," stated Hartha.

"Please, great elephant, tell me of this quest," requested Marathi.

"Oh, young Marathi, we live in a troubled land. The powerful and evil Mardosa has stolen away our king's only daughter."

"Tell me . . . is she beautiful? And what is her name?" asked Marathi excitedly.

"Her name is Orchadina, and she is just as beautiful and sweet as the orchid flower. Look up at the sky, and I will paint a picture of her beauty."

Marathi exclaimed with amazement, "Oh, she is delicately beautiful!" and then suddenly shouted, "I will save her!"

It was beginning to get dark, so Hartha decided they should rest. They slept alongside each other peacefully. That night Marathi dreamed of the Princess Orchadina.

The next day they awoke with vigor and vitality. Both were eager to start their journey. They rambled over peaks and down into valleys toward Mardosa's fortress. It was midafternoon when the sky suddenly became dark. The sun just disappeared. Marathi became cold, and he shook from the chill in the air. Hartha soothed him by saying, "Climb underneath my ear, and you will be kept warm."

They were deep in a very thick and dense forest. Marathi thought he could see eyes peeking out of the knotholes on the trees. Abruptly, a long, bumpy arm grabbed out at him, seizing a lock of his hair. Marathi gasped with fright, and Hartha roared with anguish as he tried to run but couldn't. Long, bumpy limbs were clutching his legs tightly.

Hartha exclaimed loudly, "This forest is alive! It's evil!" Marathi clung close to Hartha in fear. His heart was racing and he felt immobilized. "Quick, Marathi, listen to me. Jump down and free my legs before this forest chokes the life out of us!"

Marathi landed on the ground, removed his knife from its sheath, and quickly began to hack away at the thick stalk holding Hartha's leg. A tree began to scream, and green blood oozed out of the stalk as it fell away from its grasp. Marathi ran to Hartha's other legs and proceeded to slash until Hartha was free. With great haste Marathi climbed onto the elephant's trunk, but another vine rapidly wrapped itself around Hartha's hind leg. With a roar Hartha tore his leg free by completely pulling up the trunk of the once living, but now dead tree. The elephant broke out of the forest with astonishing speed. Trees were stretching their limbs, trying to grab the elephant or the boy, but Hartha was too fast and powerful.

Once they were far away from the living forest, Hartha stopped. They were exhausted and slept for the rest of the day and that night, too. Early the next morning they awoke well rested.

"Mardosa's fortress is only a day's journey away," Hartha said. "Shall we get started?"

"Do you think we will reach it by day's end?" inquired Marathi.

"Not with Mardosa's determination to stop us," answered Hartha.

The elephant was right. Flying through the air at awesome speed was a flock of birds. These birds were sent by Mardosa. They dove down at Marathi and Hartha, tearing at their skin and attempting to peck out their eyes. Marathi swatted at the evil, feathered creatures with his net, and Hartha whipped his tail from side to side. Birds fell to the ground, and Hartha crushed them with his huge feet. Loud squeals would alert the boy and the elephant that another attack was coming. They stood firm and courageous against the battling birds. The dark cloud of flesh eaters descended upon them seven times. Finally the last bird lay defeated on the ground. Plumage and black blood covered the ground beneath Hartha.

Marathi and Hartha were dreadfully wounded with cuts. Hartha showed Marathi how to treat his wounds with clay so they would heal quickly. Although they were both drained of strength, they knew they had to continue their trek. It was getting late, and they were painfully tired.

Night had fallen, and Hartha was finding it hard to see in the dark. Suddenly there was a slushing sound, the earth seemed to shift, and the elephant was being swallowed up by the ground! Hartha commanded Marathi to jump off his back and grab on to a tree. Marathi followed his order. This caused Hartha to sink even deeper into the quicksand. Marathi scampered down the tree to solid ground. He pulled furiously at Hartha's trunk, but it only worsened the problem. Marathi began to cry because he was helpless, and the elephant was slipping down faster and faster.

Hartha gently spoke to Marathi. "Do not grieve over me. I have lived for over three hundred years, and I am tired. I will return after a long rest. You must not stop. You must save the princess."

Marathi cried, "I can't save the princess without you!"

"Nonsense. You have proven you are a man and are quite able. Now listen to me, Marathi. There isn't much time. Take the medallion from my forehead."

Marathi stretched his arm and tugged at the medallion.

Hartha said, "It has been passed down through my race, and it holds our power. You are most worthy of it."

Marathi held the medallion tightly in his hand as Hartha disappeared. He was filled with rage and sorrow. He ran through the jungle wildly toward the evil fortress. He had known the elephant for only a few short days, but the love and trust that had grown between them were hard to find in a lifetime. In Hartha's memory he would complete the quest. Marathi ran to Mardosa's fort and slept hidden outside the walls.

The next morning at early dawn, Marathi woke to find a thick fog slowly rolling against the walls of the fortress. The only sound Marathi heard was his heart thumping out a warning. Carefully he arose. Patiently and persistently, he studied the wall with his fingertips. He found a stone that jutted out a few inches above his head. Clinging to the wall, he pulled himself up slowly and steadied himself on the foothold. Again he searched the wall for another protruding stone and found one to the right of his shoulder. As he started to pull his weight up, the rock began to falter. Marathi tugged the loose stone toward him, then pushed against it. The old wall was weak in this area, and slowly bits and pieces began crumbling. Finally the large stone plunged to the ground. Marathi held himself still and listened, but no noise came from within. He pulled himself up to the opening so that he could peek inside. Seeing that it was clear, he inched his lank body through the opening and dropped to the floor, finding himself in a long, narrow hallway.

Marathi followed the dank hallway to a large room. It had a dusky appearance and an eerie feeling about it. There was a magnificent staircase at the far end. Marathi carefully stepped from the shadows and silently scampered across the room and up the stairs.

He heard sobbing coming from a door to his left and placed his ear on the door to listen more closely.

The sobbing was definitely feminine, and he knew he had found the princess. Marathi lifted a wooden beam that secured the door. As he slowly pushed the door open, it creaked. The princess, sitting on a bed, turned around quickly, expecting to see Mardosa. She stood up and in silence began backing up to the far wall. With every step she took, the door inched open a little bit more. She peered at the doorway as the door finally swung wide enough to see Marathi staring back at her.

"Come with me quietly, Princess Orchadina. I am Marathi and have come to save you. Please don't be frightened of me. Give me your trust, and I'll give you your freedom."

They ran quickly and quietly across the hallway and to the staircase. But there stood Mardosa at the bottom of the stairs, wearing a black, hooded cape. His eyes burned like red-hot coals, and his jaw was tightly clamped with a snarling smile. A hideous chuckle came from deep in his throat, and, as he threw his arms in the air, he roared with a wicked laugh. Mardosa then waved his right arm, and the castle began to tremble.

Marathi grabbed Orchadina's hand and raced down the hallway, darting between the stones as they fell from the walls. At the end of the hall there was only a blank wall that was beginning to crack from the vigorous shaking. There was no window or doorway for escape. Marathi pushed the princess behind him and stood firm, facing Mardosa as he came toward them, step by step. Marathi drew out his knife and threw it at the evil Mardosa, only to have it disappear in thin air before it could plunge into Mardosa's chest. Marathi reached for his net and hurled it at Mardosa, but it too disappeared in thin air.

Mardosa was drawing closer and closer. With each step he chuckled deep in his throat, and his burning eyes were fixed on Marathi's throat. Marathi felt the medallion around his neck getting hotter and hotter. Hartha had told him it was powerful! He ripped the medallion from his neck and felt the power and heat in his hand. He threw it straight at Mardosa. The evil master raised his cloak for protection, but the medallion struck its target, and in a puff of smoke Mardosa disappeared.

The stones fell faster. Marathi turned to Orchadina and quickly put his arm around her shoulder and led her down the hallway. They raced over the stairs and across the large room to the outside and the rolling fog. As they were running from the castle, the trembling erupted into a tremendous shaking. The stones and rocks crashed to the earth, leaving only dust and debris where the evil fortress once stood.

Orchadina took Marathi back to her father the king. There Marathi was hailed as a hero and soon married Orchadina. Marathi later came to power and ruled the kingdom peacefully. He often told the stories of Hartha to his children as his ancestors had told the stories to him.

ABOUT THE AUTHOR

Grant Rippetoe composed this story while a student at Swampscott Jr. High School in Swampscott, Massachusetts. Currently a student at Swampscott High School, Mr. Rippetoe's interests include hockey, soccer, windsurfing, rollerskating, and reading.

The paper may be late, but the excuse is creative . . .

Another Missing Assignment

by PAUL LEBENS-ENGLAND

Hey, England!! I don't see your paper here. Is that another missing assignment?"

"Well, no, not exactly! Ya see, it's like this. I was sleeping, and our house caught on fire. And the fire spread to the natural gas spring in our garage. Yeah. So I left to go get the fire department. But they weren't home. It was the day of the Firemen's Ball. Yeah! Yeah! So I ran to my house to put the fire out with our irrigation hose. Yeah! But the irrigation water wasn't turned on yet. So I ran toward the river to get some water to put the fire out. Yeah! But on the way, an alien saucer came down from space. Little green men came out and forced me to get into their vessel. And they took me to their planet for twelve years, and they took my paper. Yeah. Then they brought me back to Earth, and it was only two hours later. Yeah! So I had to rush to school, but I fell in a roaring river. Yeah. And I was carried to the ocean where I was immediately swallowed by a whale. Yeah. Lucky me, I had a note and a bottle handy. So I floated it up to the top. Yeah! I was getting cold, but I knew I had to redo my homework. Yeah. It seemed like I was in that belly forever. So I started a small fire. Yeah. But that killed the whale. I was finally freed, but I got picked up by an Indian salmon net. Yeah. Yeah. Yeah. And they took me to their shack where they tied me to a stake and lit the fire below me. Yeah. Lucky I wrote that note in the bottle, though, because soon the Marines came to my rescue. Yeah. Yeah. And they took me to my grandparents' house so I could finally redo my homework. Yeah. So I had it done. But on my way to school, I was attacked by a giant herd of pit bulls. Yeah. And God knows I tried to hold on to my paper, but while I was holding it, my hands nearly got bitten off. Yeah. Yeah. And the dogs got my paper. I was lucky enough just to get to school."

ABOUT THE AUTHOR

Paul Lebens-England lives in Yakima, Washington, where he attends West Valley Jr. High School.

Will she know the value of what she already has?

The Black Stag

by ANIKA TORRUELLA

Xim walked slowly through the forest. The pack of wood on her back had made her shoulders sore, but she ignored the pain. She sighed because she still had nine miles before she reached home. Her thoughts turned to why she had chosen to walk eighteen miles in the first place. She had hoped to sell the oak wood on her back for a few copper pieces in town, but she could only sell enough for a smattering of brass ones. She would use the coins to buy her mother a present for All Gens Day. Xim was an only child, and when she was two her father had died of fever. They never had enough money for proper schooling, so her mother taught her at home. The small family lived too far out of the way for friends, so Xim's mother was also her best friend, not to mention being mentor and disciplinarian. She owed so much to her mother, and a few copper pieces would have made her so happy! Memories about all the things her mother was flitted happily in her mind.

Rounding the bend in the forest path that would have led her home, she noticed that something was very wrong. She had walked this path so many times that she knew it better than her own right arm, but strangely enough she did not recognize this part of the darkening woods. She walked slowly among the trees, hoping things would become more familiar, but instead of lazily curving outward, the unfaithful pathway wound deeper into the forbidding woods.

Xim was getting nowhere. She turned to retrace her steps, only to find that the trail had virtually vanished behind her! Slowly turning back, Xim saw something dance at the edge of her vision, but when she turned to look at it, it was gone. It flitted on the other side of the trail, and again the strange figure was gone. Then Xim looked straight onto the path, and the fleet figure finally revealed itself.

It was a black stag, his hide darker than a starless night, his hooves and antlers deeper in color than the most polished onyx: a vision of absolute beauty and darkness.

The stag looked at Xim, and Xim looked back into the liquid black eyes of the stag. The beautiful creature nodded his head slightly as if he had found what he was looking for; then the air around him shimmered like the heated air before a fire. Dazzled by such beauty, Xim's eyes smarted and looked away. When they could again focus, the stag was gone and there in his place stood the most beautiful woman Xim had ever seen. Xim dropped to the forest's velvet carpet in front of such incredible beauty, and slid the homely pack of wood off her sore back. The woman looked at Xim with large, almond-shaped eyes that were liquid like those of the stag, but distinctly sky blue.

"My name is Rayna," she said in a rich, throaty voice. Rayna cupped her hands before her, and her curving lips formed words Xim could not understand. The perfectly formed hands began to glow so brightly Xim could barely look at them. Finally adjusting to the light, Xim's eyes widened through the stinging tears that had begun to form. In Rayna's hands was a large crystal ball filled with gems of all shapes and colors.

"Would you like this?" Rayna asked in a voice like silk.

"More than anything," Xim breathed. This gift to her mother would be worth more than a casket of copper pieces.

"What will you give me in return?"

In return? Xim had nothing about her, except . . . her necklace was not worth much; it was made of string and braided with wire gilded in brass. It could not be worth more than a quarter brass piece, but maybe, maybe Rayna would take it. She slipped it over her head and held it out.

"My necklace?"

Rayna's eyes narrowed slightly, and she shook her glorious head. "Do you not have something of more value?"

Xim dug into her pockets once more, only to find the eight brass pieces for which she had sold some wood in the town. She held these out.

"I have eight brass pieces . . . and these oak logs."

Rayna's eyes narrowed a bit more. "No, I'm sorry; do you have nothing else?"

"Nothing," Xim said longingly as she placed the

coins back in her pocket.

Rayna's pale eyes looked her over. "Yes—you!" she said in a voice that spoke like the wind and the rain. "Many people traverse these paths, but only a few are rich enough to call me out of my solitude and trade."

Xim was puzzled; all she had, she had already offered.

Rayna smiled slightly. "It is very . . . lonesome in these woods; sometimes the earth is so quiet, you can hear the trees whisper their secrets on the wind . . . yes, it is very lonesome in these woods, and I become lonely for company. The memories you hold of your mother are like fresh, untainted air. They are the most peaceful, the most happy I have encountered in a hundred years. Will you give them to me?"

Xim looked achingly at the translucent ball in Rayna's hands. The most perfect gift was hers to take, and yet . . . she remembered the nights her mother sang her to sleep, being held in her arms while sobs shook her tiny body and her mother brushed away the tears, the smell of her faint perfume, the smile she gave Xim when she came home, the consoling hours they spent in quiet repose . . . and she knew she could not give these memories away.

"No," she said quietly, almost afraid she would regret her choice.

Rayna nodded simply and changed back to the stag that was herself. This time the stag was white, his hide the color of a full moon, and his rack like pearls.

The white stag led her slowly onto a curving path. Xim wished to talk with Rayna once more, but suddenly she heard the sound of a bird, so sweet, so pure, it pierced her very heart. When she turned to search for it, its song ceased. And when she turned back to the path, the stag was gone.

Xim ran along the now-familiar path toward her small cottage. *How strange*, she thought. *But at least we have some brass coins.* She reached into her pocket to remove the meager supply. The coins seemed heavier, she decided, and as she felt for their markings, she stopped running. For what she felt were not the shallow markings of a lemon tree, but the deep grooves of a face! She pulled the coins out and drew her breath in. She held not eight brass coins, but eight gold ones! Clutching the coins to her chest, she broke out running again. Xim burst through the small cottage door.

"Joyous Gen, Mother!" she called.

ABOUT THE AUTHOR

Anika Torruella lives in Dale City, Virginia, and attends Osbourn Park High School. She wrote this story while a student at Saunders Middle School in Manassas, Virginia. Drama, astronomy, Ancient Egypt, mythology, Ping-Pong, and "hanging around the mall" are among her favorite pastimes.

A perfect being, a fatal flaw, and a love
stronger than death . . .

Theron

by *ELLEN PERRY*

There once was a time, before the great heroes
were alive, years before the Argonauts went on
the perilous Quest for the Golden Fleece, when
the mighty god Zeus became disappointed at the wicked-
ness of all the people on Earth and decided to punish
them. He and his brother Poseidon, the powerful God
of the Sea, plotted together to send a terrible flood to
destroy mankind, but Artemis intervened. She believed
that if one man could be created flawless beyond com-
pare by the divinities, he, as king, would reform the
Earth people.

A vast meeting was held on Mt. Olympus. The great
and lesser gods participated, as did the gods of Earth.
They discussed at length the proposition made by
Artemis. Though some were a bit skeptical, the ma-
jority of the gods decided that trying it would be better than simply bringing disaster to the land all at once.

Plans took shape immediately to begin the creation

of one supreme mortal who would bring peace and good will to the people of Earth. Many of the divinities agreed that blessing the man with their own individual best traits and talents would give him many admirable characteristics. Hephaestus, God of Fire, was asked to design the face and body of the man, and he cast and shaped him from bronze. He worked painstakingly for days. When he finally finished, the blacksmith god was pleased with his endeavors; the man was beautiful, his features made perfect by flame.

Theron, as the man was named by Hestia, was brought to Mt. Olympus at once. He lay before Zeus, motionless and very handsome, on a slab of bronze. Once again, the divinities were brought together, with the exception of two. Apollo, God of Light, Music, and Poetry, was envious of the stately mortal and had no desire to contribute any of his own gifts to him. Ares, however, the murderous, cruel God of War, had been commanded by Zeus and Hera to keep away during the fashioning of the king. They and the other gods believed he had nothing worth granting Theron, which was true; he was violent and full of hatred.

Touching the statue's forehead, Athena began the ritual by instilling in Theron her gifts of wisdom, reason, and understanding. Hermes joined her, presenting Theron with his unique craftiness and wit. Artemis touched his strong arms and hands, and he was blessed with the art of the hunt. Finally, by placing her delicate hand on Theron's lifeless chest, Aphrodite warmed his cold heart and gave him a sense of love and compassion.

Zeus, who had been watching all this time from his throne, rose to his feet; the gods drew back in awe, nearly blinded by his radiance. With all the power he could muster from his mind and body, Zeus hurled a thunderbolt deep into the statue, shattering it into a shower of sparks and fire. When the smoke cleared and a colorful mist rose, Theron appeared. His eyes were a deep brown, and his hair lay in curls about his head. He was alive, the perfect mortal, a king who possessed traits of the gods themselves. Theron was a masterpiece.

The Graces fell in love with him instantly. They sacrificed themselves so that their spirits, Splendor, Mirth, and Good Cheer, would enter Theron's spirit and belong to him. Thus, he was not only a wise and skilled king, but also a loving, merry man who would teach and inspire the people of Earth. The divinities rejoiced!

What the gods did not know, however, was that Eris, the Goddess of Discord, who would later cause trouble with Paris just before the Trojan War, and Ares were scheming together. Eris devised a plan, which Ares carried out months later at a banquet in King Theron's palace.

Before the feast, while the guests were dancing merrily and the crowded ballroom was buzzing with talk and laughter, Ares crept silently into the dining hall. He placed a powerful sleeping potion, which would take effect within hours, in Theron's wine.

Some time after the grand reception, Theron found himself growing drowsy, just as Ares had intended. The king staggered into his chambers and fell into a deep, dreamless sleep. There, waiting in the shadows, stood the evil war god. Ares cut himself with a silver blade and then made a small incision in Theron's chest.

He watched as his own vile blood trickled into Theron's tiny wound. Ares sneered with satisfaction, cackling at the "gift" he had given to the king. This impeccable being now had a merciless, violent temper, and though it was only a fraction of his composition, still it was there, coursing through his veins, and would always be part of him.

Time passed, and mankind continued to improve under the rule of King Theron, companion of the Olympians. Poseidon presented him with a beautiful stallion. Even Apollo came to appreciate him. The two became great friends, and although he had been selfish and jealous before, Apollo taught Theron to play the lyre.

But Theron was closest to Artemis and was with her more than almost any other. He knew she was responsible for giving him life. She, the Goddess of the Moon, admitted to him that she was lonely in the sky at night, so Theron kept her company every time the sun disappeared by talking with her as he rested on the Earth. But still she was sad, for as she looked down upon him from her perch in the night sky, he seemed so far away.

For several years mankind prospered; everything was going according to plan. Food was plentiful, and men were generous and kind to one another. For the first time in decades, there was peace in the land. But then one day, as ominous storms brewed in the skies and thunder rolled like waves across heavy dark clouds, King Theron flew into a fit of rage over a minor conflict with a peasant and killed twenty innocent men with the blade of his sword.

The land became chaotic and immediately returned to its wicked ways. Those who at one time had faith in their king now scorned him and put on their old masks of bitter hatred and suspicion. Evil plagued the land; people cursed and even killed each other, as if to find answers to their hurting hearts' questions. Silently, Ares congratulated himself.

Theron was haunted by his conscience day and night, overcome with guilt and remorse. Deeply grieved, he locked himself in the cellar of his palace without food for many days, trying to reason with himself. He couldn't understand why he had betrayed the gods who had given him life and the people who had trusted and admired him. Finally, one dark night, he decided that he was not deserving of the life given him; with the sword that had killed so many others, he stabbed himself in the chest.

As King Theron lay dying alone in the seclusion of his damp cellar, he whispered a final wish. "Please," he called to the gods, "pity me and allow me to spend eternity with the one merciful enough to give the world a second chance. I want to comfort and love her, the lonely Goddess of the Moon, as she shines in the cold night sky."

And with these words, he died.

The Graces, who had perished to give Theron their souls, returned to life as the blood, both good and evil, spilled from his broken heart. They wept over his tranquil, beautiful body, then fled to Mt. Olympus to tell Zeus about Ares, for they had been a part of Theron and were the only ones to know the truth. The heartless, vicious god was severely punished for the heinous deed he had committed.

The Olympians mourned the loss of King Theron. Artemis in particular suffered from a heavy, anguished heart. Upon seeing her rare tears, Zeus was profoundly moved and possessed of a divine inspiration: "May the mortal king live forever in the realm of my sky near the one who loved him most!" And with these words the night burst into color, as it had the day Theron was brought to life. Sparks and flame and glittering brilliance illuminated the emptiness of the night. Theron's spirit and lifeless form were taken from the Underworld and transformed by Zeus into a million tiny shards of sparkling light. To the delight of Artemis, they were scattered like diamonds everywhere across the velvet sky.

Today, when night falls and lonely dreamers stare into space to wonder about the miracles of the universe, they sense that the moon and stars are enchanted by each other, that they laugh and talk in their own secret language until the sunlight frightens them away. They shine together on the world below to give inspiration and hope to those who will listen to their midnight love songs. Though the light of morning dims their silver radiance, the stars and moon will not be parted, and will shine together till the end of time.

ABOUT THE AUTHOR

Ellen Perry lives in Asheville, North Carolina, and attends North Buncombe High School in Weaverville, North Carolina. Her interests include playing the clarinet, running track, and involvement in Student Council and SADD.

Earth faces her worst enemies!

The Attack

by *Joseph Gallagher*

As the captain looked down, he saw the planet he was going to destroy: Earth. He had several brilliant plans in mind as to how to destroy this planet.

"First Mate Nako!" yelled the captain. Soon the first mate of the starship stood beside him.

"Yes, Captain?"

"Do you know what I'm going to do to that planet below?"

"What, Captain?"

The captain grinned and said, "I will contaminate their water supply! I'll put tons of filth in it! The sea life will die off slowly, and soon their food chain will crumble. I—"

"Excuse me, Captain, but aren't they doing that already?"

The captain frowned and said, "What?"

"Yes, Captain. Their water is already disgusting.

The land life can't even drink it in some places. They pour tons of garbage into it every day, and the sea life is already dying off. Sorry."

After a pause, the captain said, "Well, never mind, never mind. Instead, I'll destroy the invisible wall that protects them from the sun's radiation! They will all become sick, and slowly—"

"They're doing that too, sir."

"—die off! Yes, a gruesome fate in—" the captain stopped, and looked at the first mate. "What did you say?"

"They're doing it. They have been producing materials that can slowly make holes in what they call the 'ozone layer.' It gives them a deadly skin disease."

"Hmmmm . . . then . . . I'll have our spies circulate a substance that will seem to make humans happy, but will actually kill them slowly. It will be highly addictive, and soon humans will do anything for more! Then we'll move in and—"

"It's already been done, sir. A lot of humans are already addicted to many such substances, and a few humans are making a real profit off them."

"Well, for Gnob's sake, Nako!" burst out the captain. "Why are they so bent on suicide?"

"Oh, a few are trying to stop the planet's course of destruction, sir. It's just that hardly anyone listens to them."

The captain looked depressed. "Well, they've got us this time, Nako. I've run out of ideas." Suddenly a gleam came into the captain's eyes. "But wait! I have it! Listen to this, Nako! I shall LEAVE THEM ALONE!! That's it! In 1,000 years they'll have died off. What do you think of that, eh?"

"Fiendishly clever, sir," said Nako, stifling a yawn. "Give the order to turn the ship, Nako," said the captain, chuckling. The first mate gave the order, and the huge starship turned toward home.

ABOUT THE AUTHOR

Joseph Gallagher lives in Newburyport, Massachusetts. He wrote this story as a student at Immaculate Conception School, also in Newburyport.

Who created the world?

Quest for Truth

by *Jodi Triplett*

A lonely howl broke the silence, followed immediately by another, and yet another. Shivering,
the old woman latched the door and the shut-
ters against the noise. She sat down once more at her
loom and began to weave. So intent on her work was
she, that she didn't even hear someone entering.

"And what do you weave tonight?" asked a deep
voice.

"The waves of the ocean have caught the moonbeams and taken them far away; I must get them back,"
answered the old woman.

"So you weave a net?" he asked.

"Come and see," she replied. The loom revealed a
silken net, strung in the water which bobbed it gently
up and down. Inside the net lay a gossamer butterfly,
drinking nectar from a pale rose. "To lure the water,
for it loves pretty things," she explained.

"In which case you had better watch out, or it will

come for you!" laughed Eli. *It is only a strange picture on a loom*, he thought to himself, *born of this old woman's mind*.

"A loom on which I created the world and can change it," she replied, unperturbed.

"Creator of the world!" scoffed Eli. As he went back along the forest trail, he muttered to himself, "Why, everyone knows she is just a crazy old woman who thinks she created the world." Comforted, he went on.

Another howl sounded, very close to where Eli was walking. Suddenly, a dozen gray shadows were about him. Flickering yellow eyes regarded him calmly.

"Hello," said Eli gravely.

A voice deep with age and wisdom replied, "Why did you go there?"

"I don't know why exactly," he said, "but she thinks she created the world."

A sound which was surprisingly like laughter passed through the pack of wolves. "Why," said the voice, "that is impossible since it was I and my pack who made the world."

"Then why did you make humans?" asked Eli, mystified.

"A mistake," was the sad reply. The wolves were gone as quickly as they had come, and Eli proceeded on.

A gentle river flowed quietly past him, visiting the sea. Eli asked the river if she had seen any moonbeams. "Here," the melodic, slurred voice of the river said. A patch of light made the river dance. "But the ocean has stolen all the rest away!" Eli did not know what to do, and began to walk on, but the river called him back.

"Wait!" she pleaded. "I know what you are thinking," she said. "I know I was foolish to create the ocean, who is selfish, but I know I made a mistake."

"Then why can't you simply take it away, if you created the world as you imply?" asked Eli.

"I cannot, for it is against life itself. But the flowing of my tears makes the ocean salty, so you know that I grieve for my mistakes."

Puzzled, Eli walked on and the river did not try to stop him. "Everyone says they created the world; I wonder who really did?" he mused.

"Why of course everyone knows I did," said a gravelly voice.

"Who said that?" demanded Eli.

"I did," replied the voice, directly underfoot. The path on which he was walking was the speaker. "I direct the lives of all my creations by making a place for them to see where they are going," continued the path.

"What happens if someone strays from the path?" questioned Eli.

"I am always here for them to come back to," was the reply.

"I don't believe you," Eli said. "Everyone keeps telling me this."

Angry, the path disappeared. Eli said he was sorry and asked if the path would please come back. The path came back immediately and led him on without comment down a dew-soaked hill. Grass grew lushly on either side of him and distant hills overhung the scene. A fine mist hung low over the hills, adding an ethereal quality.

"I can show you all the beauties of the world," the path said, and Eli agreed, looking about him.

A sudden image in Eli's mind of the silken net made

him ask if the path knew of any moonbeams.

"The sea took them, stole them from me!" The path disappeared, and no coaxing on Eli's part could get it back.

Eli walked on, and soon his feet were soaked. The distant sound of water led him on, and soon salty spray clung delicately to his face. The slight mist turned into a heavy fog which obscured his vision. The sandy beach upon which he trod wound around the hills, patiently enduring the steady abuse of pounding ocean waves. A large wave broke spitefully over his knees and Eli angrily informed the ocean that everything he had heard about it was true. The ocean stilled suddenly, making everything quiet.

"And just what have you heard?" demanded its gruff voice.

"That you are selfish, and turned against your creators, going even so far as to steal the beautiful moonbeams," replied Eli.

"Humph. That's not true at all! The rivers all come to me—I don't force them here—and I always give some of myself to the clouds so the rivers may stay flowing. As for turning against my creators, how could I when I created everything?"

"Well—" began Eli.

"And moonbeams," the ocean swept on, ignoring his rather lame beginning, "the moonbeams play across me all the time; I have not stolen them. They come and go."

Suddenly, the ocean began to churn violently. Eli backed up, alarmed.

"No!" cried the ocean. "No, you cannot take them!"

Eli turned and saw the old woman. In her hands

lay a silken net, parted just enough to reveal a butterfly and a single rose.

"No," repeated the ocean in an anguished voice. Unperturbed, the old woman cast her net and waited. Huge waves broke over the beach in an effort to shake off the net, but the net bobbed indifferently in the water. The fog thinned as a faint outline of the sun appeared in the distant hills. Moonbeams fluttered gently across the ocean, ready to leave, and then saw the net. The beams gently reached for the butterfly and were caught. Pale morning light streamed across the water and the moonbeams were gone. The old woman calmly handed Eli the net and told him to set them free far away from the ocean, or it would take them again. She left, and Eli was left alone except for the quiet weeping of the grieving ocean.

Eli went on, but the crying of the ocean could be heard long after he could no longer see it. The sun was still low in the sky, laboring to bring warmth. He paused against an outcropping of rock to rest.

"Why, I haven't seen the likes of this in ages!" exclaimed a hoarse voice.

"Magic," agreed another.

"I'm sorry," the first voice said, seeing Eli. "I am Jorfin, creator of the world."

"And I am Filina, who has to put up with this tiring old fool."

Eli looked more closely and found that the two who had spoken were the massive outcroppings of rock upon which he sat and a slender fir tree.

"Magic?" Eli began.

"Never mind now, go on and it will become clear in time." Eli resignedly walked on.

He was tired, and weeds held him back from his way. Eli suddenly remembered the path and called for it. "Of course I am here," the path spoke up, and Eli walked on contentedly. "As I was saying before, I will show you all the places of beauty."

That afternoon was one that Eli would not soon forget. The path led him through clear, meandering brooks and tall, ancient forests. Snowcapped mountains and lonely ridges were silhouetted in the distance. Ponds held plump frogs that sang of summer. Eagles screamed of the fierce joy of the kill, and foxes spoke of sly tricks and cleverness. Grass swayed gently under the silent shadows of the setting sun, and trees whispered of ancient, untold years. The wonder of the forest told a beautiful, yet forbidding story. "I can lead you nowhere else," said the path, and was gone.

Eli proceeded, alone but for the silken net which he clutched tightly to his chest, and came upon a small clearing. Leaning against a tree, he suddenly realized how tired he was. Remembering the moonbeams, he opened the net. In the gathering dusk, the moonbeams streaked beautifully into the sky.

Beneath the bright beams, Eli suddenly saw clearly. Far off, in the heavens, he could hear laughter as the creator of the world examined Eli's journey and found it humorous.

ABOUT THE AUTHOR

Jodi Triplett lives in Cheney, Washington, and is a student at Cheney Jr. High School. Horseback riding, debate, volleyball, and basketball are some of Jodi's hobbies, along with collecting works of fantasy and science fiction.

A lesson in harmony . . .

Song of Masefield

by *MICHELLE DIVITO*

I never met a horse I didn't like," a man once said. Well, that can mean only one thing—he never met Masefield.

Masefield was a horse like many in the meadow, with gorgeous brown shiny hair and a beautiful black mane and tail. He frolicked in the grasslands and galloped through the thousands of acres of alfalfa and bluegrass just like all the other horses of the land. You could find him feasting on lush green grass or sipping from deep blue pools of water between steep hills and in natural trenches after a rain.

There was a difference, however, for all the other animals of the meadow were kind, friendly, and supportive, but not Masefield. He teased the unfortunate and was downright mean. On one occasion, Masefield spotted a squirrel in need of assistance. The poor thing was hanging from a limb, trying desperately to grasp a single plump acorn. Each time he lunged, there was still a gap of several inches between him and the acorn. "Silly Chesterton," Masefield taunted in that boisterous voice of his. "Can't you see you are too short and fat to reach that worthless acorn you're after? Why, you don't have the ingenuity to get it! I, of course, could grab it with no trouble at all." And though he easily could have helped, Masefield went on his way, leaving Chesterton with such a strong desire for the nut that he burst into tears.

Now, one would think that Masefield, being the horse he was, did not deeply care for anything in the world. This wasn't true. There was one thing in life Masefield did cherish: singing.

Each morning he would wake up and excitedly race to the edge of the forest where the bright young sun was just beginning to paint the sky. This part of the wood was where the canaries nested, and each dawn was like a symphony of melodies. Masefield relished this event every day. He would sit quite still in the center of a cluster of trees, close his eyes, and try to catch each beautiful sound the canaries uttered.

Masefield craved the ability to sing so much that sometimes it was painful. He had such a want, but not a thread of hope. The knowledge that someone could do something better than he was unacceptable to him. Masefield would try to sing, practicing for hours, but he would soon realize how horrible his sounds were and become discouraged, frustrated, and angry.

One morning when he was feeling particularly inspired by the songs of the canaries, Masefield worked his way into the depths of the forest where he was sure no animal roamed and began his practice. It was dreadful! Every note was off-key, every sound scratchy.

Masefield, absorbed in his work, was unaware of an observer sitting quietly on a branch of the elm tree next to him. It was a small, frail, and extremely old canary who thought the awful racket quite amusing. Not noticing the bird, Masefield kept practicing. But soon enough, the canary rustled the still leaves of the tree and Masefield stopped abruptly. "Who is there? Who's listening?" Masefield cried in an embarrassed tone.

"No need to be ashamed, young horse. It is only Asbury."

"Asbury, Asbury!" Masefield blustered. "Why, you have no right to be here! And how dare you listen to my songs!"

There was no reply. At least not immediately. Then Asbury calmly responded, "I suppose if that's your attitude, I cannot be of help to you."

Masefield thought a moment, and just as Asbury was about to take flight, he shouted, "Wait! What is it you wish to say? I suppose I will hear you."

Asbury replied, "You struggle to sing, but all along you have been capable of doing so. You are a horse and have only the ability to sing like a horse. You are not a canary. Only *they* can make the songs of canaries. Be what you are, because what you are can be beautiful. Do not be frustrated because the sound from your lips is not the music of dawn. Change your song from the hopeless chirps of a birdlike horse to the melodies of a stallion."

Masefield, who had never been spoken to in such a manner, thought about what the old bird had said. He realized that Asbury was right. He had been foolish in trying to imitate the canaries. "Thank you, old bird, for leading me in the right direction. I'll work on your suggestion."

That night Masefield began his efforts anew, not trying to be something he wasn't, but singing like a horse. His songs were gorgeous, not canary-gorgeous, but horse-gorgeous. He was finally satisfied.

The next morning, Masefield went as usual to the edge of the wood to listen to the canaries sing their sweet melodies. As he listened, the music held him spellbound, and he began to sing his beautiful horse songs. The birds stopped, but Masefield did not. The canaries listened awhile, then one or two joined in, a bit uncertain. Eventually all the rest of the birds were participating, Masefield singing a beautiful horse song, the canaries singing their unique bird tune. It was the most beautiful, harmonic music Masefield had ever experienced.

Afterwards, the canaries invited Masefield to their nightly chorus. "Every night some of the animals of this land meet at the water's edge and have a beautiful concerto with hundreds of different sounds that blend into a beautiful work of art," a canary informed him. (This activity had been kept from Masefield because of his mean disposition.)

All this sounded so good to Masefield! Being a part of a chorus was unbelievable to him. *I will be the best! I will sing better than anyone there*, he thought to himself.

After sunset, Masefield headed out to the water's edge. The moon was full and its light guided him all the way there. He met hundreds of different animals, all there for the same reason. What a sight! Turtles, snakes, frogs, mice, birds, rabbits, deer, ponies, and just about every other kind of animal was present. All were thought by Masefield to be inferior to him. The canaries were there, with Asbury in the lead, and so was Chesterton, the squirrel Masefield had taunted only days before.

When the music began, Masefield was almost knocked over with astonishment. Every animal there sang in its own way, and each was unique and beautiful. There were frog songs, turtle songs, mice songs, and on and on. Masefield saw how each animal needed the other to create harmony, and at last he understood that it is the same in life. He saw himself as part of life's chain—just one link, no better than the others, yet vital.

They sang through the night, and, as the animals were leaving, they noticed a smile on Masefield's face and a twinkle in his eyes. All the animals knew that he and the forest would never be the same. And indeed they never were.

ABOUT THE AUTHOR

Michelle DiVito lives in Glenview, Illinois, where she is a student at Glenbrook South High School. Besides writing, she enjoys volleyball, skiing, and swimming. "Song of Masefield" was written while Miss DiVito attended Springman Jr. High School in Glenview.

A tale of star-crossed lovers.

The Story of the Aurora Borealis

by JAMIE PFLASTERER

Riotous laughter broke the night's calm and shook Mt. Olympus. Bacchus, god of wine and revelry and thus the favorite of the gods, had come to visit. As was Bacchus's nature, he had turned the rather dull gathering into a roaring Bacchanalia. It seemed as though his mere presence was intoxicating. Jove, leader of the gods, was out of control, which wasn't unusual according to Juno, his wife. He was running around with a huge chalice sitting upside down on his head and was flirting with all the goddesses. Neptune, god of the sea and Jove's brother, was accidentally sticking people with his trident while describing a fierce battle with an immense, bottom-dwelling killer whale.

However, not everyone was joining in the fun. Sol, former god of the sun; Luna, former goddess of the moon; and Aurora, goddess of dawn, dubbed "The Titan Triples," sat demurely in the corner. Sol and Luna were there only because of perfunctory courtesy on the part of Jove and Juno. Since Saturn, former leader of the gods, and the Titans, his followers, had been overthrown by the Olympians, Apollo and Diana were regarded as the true god and goddess of the sun and moon, respectively. However, no one replaced Aurora as the goddess of dawn. She was a favorite among the Olympians. Rumor had it that she nearly rivaled the looks of Venus, goddess of love and beauty, when she smiled. However, that was rare since the terrible incident with Tithonus, Aurora's former lover.

Aurora had fallen in love with Tithonus, a mortal man, many thousands of years ago. She had taken up Tithonus from Earth, and they lived together at Aurora's home near World's End. Aurora knew, however, that their wonderful relationship couldn't last because Tithonus was mortal and would eventually grow old and die. She went before Jove and, using all of her charm, got him to agree to grant her one wish. She asked for eternal life for Tithonus, and her wish was granted. Poor Aurora, she forgot to ask also for his eternal youth! So Tithonus still lives; however, he has gotten quite old, and over the years he has shrunk and shriveled down into the form of a grasshopper. Aurora has been in constant mourning for him since, and has never loved another.

Aurora was quite shy. At the Bacchanalia, she had veiled herself in clouds and mists so that none of her could be seen, and she would barely speak to anyone who tried to coax her out of her little corner.

Suddenly, a chill spread throughout the vast room. Everyone turned around to see who had ushered in such an ill omen, and they all immediately relaxed again. Boreas, god of the north wind, had entered. It was only natural that one such as he brought a chill wherever he went. However, the feeling of unease never quite left the room.

Boreas floated around the room, lightly dusted with frost and rime. Great icicles hung from his hair and clothes. He exchanged pleasantries with Jove and his court and then sat down on the fringe of the crowd. Unlike Aurora and Bacchus, Boreas was not a favorite of the gods. It was not that he was bad-mannered or unpleasant. He was simply too cold and distant for many people's tastes. Boreas didn't mind this. In fact, he preferred to be left to his own devices. He settled himself down in a chair and watched all the fun.

The gods and goddesses finally began to calm down and were becoming bored. As they were looking around for something else to amuse them, Proserpine, the young, carefree goddess of spring, spotted Aurora. "Sing for us!" she pleaded. "Call the dawn!"

Aurora looked away shyly, but a collective cry went up for her. Finally she walked demurely to the center of the room. The mists lifted, revealing a seemingly young girl clad in a simple homespun tunic. However, this young girl possessed an unearthly beauty. Aurora took a deep breath, opened her mouth, and began to sing.

Contrary to popular opinion, the dawn is not the rosy fingertips of Aurora. Instead, Aurora uses an ancient melody, older than time itself, to beckon the dawn back from its nighttime hiding place. Aurora weaves her powerful magic within the song itself and calls for the dawn to come back to Earth again.

All those sitting there were reminded of home and

their childhood as they listened to the song. A feeling
of peace and security washed over the whole group.
Then, right at the climax of the song, the first rays of
light glittered across the land. Everyone hushed and
simply took a moment to drink in the dawn and hold
on to the memory of the song.

Aurora blushed deeply; everyone stared at her as
she rushed back to her seat and again summoned the
cloaking mists about her.

"Good gods!" Boreas exclaimed in wonder. "Never
in all my years have I heard or witnessed anything so
lovely!" Aurora's song had touched something deep
inside him. He had fallen in love with her.

Apollo, god of youth, medicine, the sun, and music, among other things, was leaning on the wall next
to him. He chuckled. "No doubt many of the others
gathered here are saying the same thing. Although I
am the god of music, she rivals even me at my best."

"Who is she?" Boreas breathed in awe.

"Don't you know? That was Aurora, goddess of
dawn. She lives away from Mt. Olympus at the edge
of the world."

"Of course, now I remember!" Boreas was silent
for a moment, lost in thought. Finally he said, "Apollo,
I need your help."

Apollo drew his attention back to Boreas. "How
may I assist?"

Boreas had formulated a plan to get Aurora's love.
Now all he needed was Apollo's help. "Can you make
me Aurora's equal in song?"

Apollo grinned. "You should be consulting Venus
on matters of love instead of me." Boreas flushed. Serious
now, Apollo frowned, "This is no small thing you're

asking for."

Boreas looked panicked. "Please help me! I will repay you in any way I can!"

Apollo thought for a moment and then said brightly, "Could you trade me two of your coldest winds to keep me cool as I drive the chariot of the sun across the sky, in exchange for changing your voice?"

Boreas quickly agreed, even though his supply of winds was limited. Apollo then slowly began to change Boreas's voice to that of a great singer. In the process he also made Boreas taller and more handsome and godlike in appearance. Finally, the change was complete. Boreas thanked Apollo soundly. "I can never repay you for what you have done."

Apollo winked at him, "Good luck!"

Boreas saw the clouded goddess get up to leave. He pushed his way through the throng of gods and goddesses, trying not to lose Aurora. Outside Mt. Olympus, he saw Aurora, or rather, the stray mists trailing along behind her. It seemed that he followed her for an endless time, always trying to keep her in sight and yet afraid to let her see him. Finally, she came to a cottage, modest by the standards of the gods. He didn't follow her inside, although he wanted to. He was too nervous to actually try to meet her face to face that night. He needed some time to think everything through once more. The sun had set hours ago, so Boreas prepared himself for a night outdoors—nothing unusual for the god of the north wind.

When Boreas awoke, the sun had not yet risen. It was obvious that Aurora was not yet awake. Boreas was trying to think of a way to sweep her off her feet, or even to just talk to her. Suddenly, he saw her walk outside and face World's End. As if it were the most natural thing in the world, the two began singing simultaneously, calling the dawn together. Melody and harmony mixed smoothly as the two sang. After seemingly an eternity, the sun rose, and both ended the song. Aurora looked at Boreas with love in her eyes, and he knew that this was only the start of their happiness. However, at that same moment, a chill wind caressed the two, causing both of them to shiver and make signs of warning against evil omens.

After many months the Olympians noticed that the sunrise was changing. The dawn seemed dimmer and paler, somehow even colder. After a few more months, the changes were much more pronounced. The dawn had definitely taken on a sickly greenish tint. Concerned, Jove summoned Aurora and Boreas to Mt. Olympus.

There was quite a commotion as Aurora entered the great hall. Aurora had also changed because she was the personification of the dawn. She looked wan, much thinner, and her skin had taken on a deathly pallor. Horrified, Luna and Sol rushed to her side. "Why, she's as cold as ice!" they exclaimed. "What have you done to her?" they demanded of Boreas.

"I haven't done anything to her!" Boreas said defensively. "I love her!"

"Boreas hasn't done anything to harm me," Aurora protested.

"But what else could have caused this condition?" Jove asked. "It is your very nature, Boreas. The dawn was never meant to be kept cold and secluded. Instead, the dawn should be warm and giving."

"I won't be parted from Boreas!" Aurora exclaimed. "If you separate us, the sun will never rise again!"

"Now, Aurora," Juno scolded. "You can hardly go on much longer in your present condition. Jove and I propose that you visit Boreas only at night at his home in the North. During the day, you must stay at your home near World's End." Sadly, Aurora and Boreas left the great hall. They went their separate ways, promising each other to meet that night at Boreas's home in the North.

Aurora visited Boreas every evening at his home. Because they both loved calling the dawn together, they still sang the ancient song, even during the night when the sun couldn't come back to the Earth. So, rather than dawn, the northern lights, or northern dawn, came instead. And ever since that time we have had the northern lights, or aurora borealis, named after Aurora and Boreas, lovers who are as different as day and night.

ABOUT THE AUTHOR

Jamie Pflasterer is a resident of Tremont, Illinois, where he attends Tremont High School. His extracurricular activities include volleyball, speech, and the duties of secretary for his church's youth board. In his spare time, Mr. Pflasterer enjoys reading and entertaining the family dog.

A tale about living, growing, and saying goodbye.

Billy the Seed

by JENNIFER BERTRAM

Billy the Maple Seed started out as nothing. His mother wanted him to grow, so she protected Billy and his brothers and sisters with her powerful limbs and root system. Each day, she made sure that her little seeds got enough sunlight, not too much, not too little. When it rained, she gave out water equally to everyone, never favoring one seed over another. All her seedlings trusted her, and there was rarely arguing over who got more of what.

"Listen, dears. Listen very carefully to my story," Billy's mother said one day. There were a few grunts and murmurs, but soon, all twelve little seeds were looking up at their mother, patiently waiting for her story. Mother's stories were fun to hear. She sometimes told of grasshoppers she had met, or robins that she had housed, but their favorites were about all the interesting plants that she had grown up with. One time she told of a foreign plant that grew only a few feet away. That plant was sassy! Always talking about how great she was and how she could survive anything—little did that plant know! She was soon cut down by Man, and no one ever saw her again.

"Once upon a time," Billy's mother began, "there was a tiny seed, not much bigger than any of you. She lived on a tree, not too much bigger than I am. She had three brothers and two sisters, but they didn't live as close together as you do. In fact, she never met a single one of her brothers. Her closest sibling was about nine inches away. This meant her mother had to care for each seed separately."

"Wow!" said Billy. "How awful!" Billy didn't know if he could have lived through dandelion pox without the support of his older brother and sister, who had it at the same time he did.

"The wind was blowing very hard one day," his mother continued. "It was awful. The little seed was holding on for dear life. She twisted and turned, but didn't fall. She heard her mother call, 'Let go! It's all right!' But the little seed was afraid. She didn't want to leave. She wanted to stay right there, in the comfort of her tree. At last she could not hold on any longer. She flew away from her home in the tree.

"My children, that little seed was me. All seeds are blown away from their homes. It is a challenge we must all face. When the time comes that you will be blown from me, you will bury yourselves in the ground, and eventually grow. You will face many obstacles, but you must never give up. It will be hard in the world, but don't be afraid."

Her children were awed. They did not want to leave her, but they nodded. The big tree smiled and patted her children on their heads.

"Mommy," asked Billy. "Why can't I stay here? It will be hard out there, you said so yourself."

"No one can stay. You know the Laws of Nature," said the mother.

Billy knew. Law #2 said: Do not stay where you aren't needed. Billy never understood until now. It was obvious he wasn't needed.

"I don't like the Laws of Nature," said Billy, snuggling up to his mother's branch. "I want to stay here with you, and never leave. I like it here. I like your stories. I like . . ." he murmured as he dozed off to dreamland.

Two days later, the wind began to blow, just as their mother had predicted. Sarah, the eldest, was the first to be blown away.

"Mommy! Help me!" cried Sarah. She was struggling to hold on. She nearly flew away but . . . she was still holding. She hadn't gone yet. She was about to lose hold. *One more blow and I'm a goner*, she thought.

Snap! They all heard it.

"Goodbye, my Sarah," said her mother with an ache in her heart.

Next, Billy's brother Joseph blew away. His fight was brief, but hard. He let go, then was able to capture another branch, but then, just as quickly, he was blown from that, too. "Mommy, I love you," he said, his voice fading as he blew away.

"Goodbye, Joseph!" she cried.

My turn's next, thought Billy. He could feel himself shaking. He didn't want to leave, but he knew he had to. "I think I'm going, Mom. I love you. Never forget me, please, Mom!" Billy tried to act brave to set a good example for his younger brothers and sisters.

"You are brave, Billy," his mother said. "I love you, and I'll never forget you. Goodbye."

Billy let loose. "Bye-bye, Mommy," he cried as he blew away.

Wow, he thought. *I'm traveling so fast!* The world seemed to be passing so quickly before him. He had never felt so free before. His sister Dawn flew by.

"Helloooo, Billy," she called.

"Helloooo, Dawn," he called back.

Oof! He had hit the ground. *Now I bury myself*, he thought. *How does one go about burying oneself? Hmmmmmmm.*

Though Billy had never tried such a thing, he managed to bury himself. He figured out how, and believe me, it took a lot out of the little seed.

First he took a deep breath and held it for as long as he possibly could. While doing this, he had to somehow make all his insides rise to his head! When he let out his breath, he was able to push down a little farther. At the exact same moment, he let all his insides drop. Each time he tried this process, he became very sleepy.

Finally he was covered with a thin layer of dirt. Exhausted, he went to sleep. He had worked very hard that day and was glad to rest.

Billy woke up the next morning to find a friend.

"Hello. My name is Myra," the new friend said.

"My name is Billy," he said shyly.

"I'm an acorn. That's an oak tree seed. What are you?"

"I'm a maple seed."

"A squirrel brought me here. How did you get here?"

"I blew in on the wind."

A soft, gentle rain began to fall. "Mmmm, that feels good," said Billy.

"It sure does," said Myra. "It'll help us grow big and strong."

All that afternoon it rained. That evening, as he drifted off to sleep, Billy thought, *I'm anxious to talk to Myra tomorrow. She seems so smart. I wonder if she knows about those harsh troubles Mom talked about.*

The next morning Billy woke up with a banging headache. Myra was crying. "Help, Billy, help!" she cried. "The squirrel's got me . . ."

Alas! Her cry was too late. Myra was being carried off by the squirrel. Billy wanted to help her. He wanted to jump out of the ground and save her, but at that moment, he was scared, too scared to open his eyes. The vision of Myra's frightened face, struck with terror! Her horrible cry for help and the murderous sounds the squirrel made when pulling her out and placing her between his teeth! The thought struck him that that could have been him.

"Oh, d-d-dear," Billy moaned. "I don't want that to happen to me!"

Billy felt his head. There was a crack in it. *Good! I must be sprouting*, he thought. *Mom sure is smart.*

Billy felt alone. No Mom. No Myra. Nobody.

Humph, thought Billy, sticking out his lower lip. "No one here," he said aloud. "No one."

"I'm here," said a deep voice.

"Who are you?" asked Billy, looking at a dirty pink tube. The thing elongated, which startled Billy for a moment. Then he realized that it was a way for the thing to move along. Billy said, "I never saw you before."

"I'm Bert. I'm a worm. A bird took my friend. I'm scared, but I try to grow anyway. I always remember my mom when I feel discouraged. Well, I must go. See ya around," said Bert.

Billy thought about that and remembered his mom. He began to push and grow.

This is hard, he thought. *Mom did this too. She had to work hard to get big, and that's what I must do.*

Soon he was big enough to peek out of the ground. Then he saw his mother!

"Mommy, Mommy," he cried. He was so small and his voice so far away that she didn't hear him. Oh, how he wanted to grow so she could see him!

As he grew he looked at the world around him. He looked at the grass, the insects, the flowers. Everything was so beautiful and exciting. *I'm so glad I'm alive*, he thought.

Before he knew it, he'd grown big enough for his mother to see him. They were so happy to see each other!

He had much to tell his mother. "I made a friend, Myra, but a squirrel took her away. And Bert, a worm. I saw so many beautiful flowers and insects."

"Oh, Billy, I'm so glad you're here. You've grown so tall!" she sighed. "But you're still not perfectly safe yet, Billy," she warned. "Please watch out for birds and rabbits. Now rest, Billy. I love you."

It wasn't long before he realized why his mother warned him about birds. All of a sudden a bird came by and pecked at the ground below Billy's slender trunk.

"Help, help!" cried Bert. The bird had Bert clenched

in his beak! How could he? Well, Billy wasn't going
to let that bird hurt his only friend!

Billy rustled his branches and yelled, "Put him down!
Put him down!" Then he reached down and swatted
the bird.

"Awk!" The bird let go of Bert, flapped his wings
at Billy, and flew away.

In the tussle, Billy had been pulled partially out of
the ground. He was very weak. "Mommy, Mommy,"
he called.

His mother woke up. "What happened?" she asked.

"A bird got me," he said weakly. "Oh, Mom, I tried!"

"Stop it! Pull yourself up. You can live," she demanded.

"I can't," he said.

"Yes, you can," his mom said.

"I will help you, Billy," Bert said. "You risked your
life for me."

Bert pushed him up. "Dig in your roots, Billy," Bert
ordered.

Billy did. "Hey, I can stand," he said. "I can live!"
All the plants cheered.

For the next few years, Billy grew and grew. Billy
the Seed had grown into a tall, strapping maple tree
and was very happy. Soon a tree named Cassandra
grew up next to him. They hit it off right away and
had 16 children: Dawn, Rachel, Brian, Karen, Michael,
Hanna, Haley, Romolo, Henry, Crystal, Sherry, David,
Linda, Jim, Lee, and Jo-Ann. All were blown away in
the same way that Billy was, and each one lived.

When Billy was 110, and Cassandra was 100, a tornado hit the forest where they lived. The tornado van-
quished the entire forest. Both Billy and Cassandra

were uprooted.

All was not lost, however. Two men came to inspect the destruction.

"I think this here tree would make some mighty fine lumber," exclaimed one, pointing to Billy.

"Ab-ser-lute-ly. This here one next to it, too," said the other, pointing to Cassandra.

"I think I'll take this tree home for the missus and make her a handsome table, if ya don't mind."

"Course not! Don't mind at all. I'm takin' the other to make a jungle gym for my young'uns."

ABOUT THE AUTHOR

Jennifer Bertram lives in Belleville, Illinois, where she attends Belleville Township High School. She wrote this story while a student at Blessed Sacrament School, also in Belleville. A dedicated musician, Miss Bertram has been playing piano since third grade and has recently taken up the violin and flute. Other creative outlets include singing in the Masterworks Chorale, dramatic performances, and giving speeches. She hopes to become a veterinarian.

Larger than life in every way . . .

Greedy Grant

by DEBRA CSEH

Back in the Old West there was a very greedy gold miner called Greedy Grant. He was born the son of a cattle rustler, who was the best in the West at the time. He got his name because he was so greedy that no one could share the same area of land within a hundred miles in any direction. He was also a giant and stood at about two hundred feet tall.

Long ago, he was out in the area that is now known as Arizona. He had heard that there was good mining there. He just picked a spot and started digging with his hundred-foot-long shovel.

About five days later, he had a huge supply of gold. But Greedy Grant just had to keep on digging to get still more gold. He had already created a huge hole, but he wanted even more gold. He never quit. What he dug would eventually become known as the Grand Canyon.

Nobody knows what became of Greedy Grant. For

all they know, he is still digging. If anybody ever notices the Grand Canyon getting deeper, it's probably just Greedy Grant, still searching for gold.

ABOUT THE AUTHOR

Debra Cseh lives in Dale City, Virginia. She wrote this story while attending Saunders Middle School in Woodbridge, Virginia.

A new legend of the Old West!

It Ain't Over Till the Fat Lady Flings

by JEFF WALD

I suppose livin' in the Old West has its advantages. You lead a good life, ridin' horses, fightin' in saloons, an' shootin' up dudes. Then you die a legend by gettin' shot in the back or bein' hung from the gallows. I got the livin' part right, but I couldn't even die right. This is an account of my death.

When I stepped into that ole Texas saloon in 1893, the only things I owned was things I had on me at the time: an ole dusty hat, my only change'a clothes, a leather coin purse, a belt'a bullets round my waist, an' my trusty six-shooter. Bein' the fastest gun in all'a Texas had its advantages, like women flockin' 'round you like chickens to their feed an' the respect of people everywhere ya went, 'specially the bartenders!

I had never been in this saloon before, but it was like all the rest: a wooden bar, wooden stairs leadin' up to the "house of ill repute," an' gamblin' tables set up all round the wooden planks of floor. I moseyed up to the bar, leaned against the brass rail, an' rapped on the top of the wooden bar with my knuckles to get the bartender's attention.

"Bartender! Bartender!" I called out. "Get me a beer!"

"Yes, sir!" he replied. I realized he knew who I was from his tone of voice, seeming nervous an' privileged at the same time.

He brought me the draft and I held it out in my hand to the smokey room around me. "Cheers to me!" I exclaimed. As I was about to take a swig, I heard a shrill gunshot from across the room and my mug shattered into a thousand pieces. Shards of glass scattered across the floor. I turned round only to find, to my surprise, the ugliest polecat I'd ever seen in my life. He was all dressed in black with a five o'clock shadow to cover his pitted face, and he had a six-shooter in his hand. He was what you might call your standard bad man: a desperado, a no-brains dude.

"You lookin' fer a heap'a trouble, stranger?" the cutthroat blurted out. A smirk came across my face.

"No." I yanked out my gun, pulled the trigger, and shot the gun outta his hand. I didn't even blink. He looked at the gun on the floor, looked at his hand, looked at me, an' stepped back through the swingin' doors. I heard the footsteps of his boots runnin' across the wooden planks outside an' then on the soft dirt of the street. I twirled my sixer round my finger a couple'a times an' put it back into its home. *Yee-hah! This is the life*, I thought.

"Oooooooo . . ." I heard from above. I looked up to see a bevy of beautiful women from the "house of ill repute." They were all wide-eyed an' full of excitement. I stepped down from the footrail an' ambled on over, directly below 'em. Giggles descended.

"I want the purdiest one'a you gals," I remarked. More giggles. Then a confused mumble as the ugliest, homeliest, fattest, roundest pork of a woman I had ever seen stepped forward. Her dress was way too small an' was splittin' at the seams.

"Here I am! The prettiest girl here . . . Catch me!"

Before I could say anything, that beast of a woman was up on the rail an' had flung herself through the air directly over the place where I stood. The last thing I saw was her shadow, an' the last thing I heard was a thud.

The funeral was short, but sad. Most of the mourners was women. There was no purdy flowers like at them normal funerals, but then again, I ain't normal. I was put in an old wooden casket, 'bout half a foot thick, my six-shooter stickin' straight up outta my folded hands (they didn't have no beads). Oh, sure, y'all probably don't even believe I exist. But if you ever happen to go to the town of Lubbock, Texas, you'll find my gravestone. Wade Boken. An' just remember the inscription, which is also a word of advice: It ain't over till the fat lady flings, so better watch out where you're standing.

ABOUT THE AUTHOR

Jeff Wald lives in Eau Claire, Wisconsin, where he is a student at Eau Claire Memorial High School.

Déjà Vu

by CARMEN NOBEL

All the children had arrived, so the Sunday school teacher began the story. She was reading from the *New Children's Bible*, a book which made the Bible interesting and easy to understand for the children. She sometimes read from the *First Children's Bible*, but the children seemed to like the stories from the *New* better.

"Once there was a man," began the teacher, when she saw a child's hand go up.

"What, Luella?" She smiled patiently.

"Is this a true story?" the child asked.

"Yes," said the teacher. "All of the stories from the *New Children's Bible* are true. We know that for a fact."

She continued. "The man's name was Noah, and he was a good man. God loved Noah, but, unfortunately, He felt that Noah was the only good man. God felt there was only one thing to do. He called Noah one day."

"On the teph-alone?" a child asked.

The teacher ignored this. "God told Noah that there would be a great destruction in which everyone would die. But God told Noah that if he followed His directions, Noah wouldn't die.

"First Noah had to build a ship. This ship would save him and his family. Then Noah had to collect two of each kind of animal on the Earth. They were to go on the ship, too. God wanted all of them to start a new world after everyone else had died.

"Noah did what God told him to, and soon God called him again: 'Now is the time, Noah,' He bellowed.

"And Noah and all the animals hurried into the ship. The ship was launched. Noah looked out of the ship and saw . . . well, what do you think he saw, children?"

"A lot of rain?" a boy asked.

"No, Raymond, that's in the *First Children's Bible*. That was another Noah. This Noah saw the Earth below him. He saw two explosions and two mushroom-shaped clouds. The great destruction had begun. Noah would have to find a new place to live." The teacher closed the book.

"And that's why we live here, teacher, and not on Earth, right?" Luella asked.

"That's right."

ABOUT THE AUTHOR

Carmen Nobel lives in Gorham, Maine. She wrote this story as a student at Gorham High School.

Not just another barroom story!

Unhappy Hour

by KERRY MITCHELL

Oscar Neville looked around the bar in disgust. *By the Bhagwan's eye, how did I get myself stuck on this backwater planet?* he thought to himself. *Dingy little bar in a dirty, scum-swamp colony. They can't even brew a decent beer.*

He turned around. Someone new had entered the bar. The man was pale and haggard, as if he had just come from a long trip. He wore the grease-stained clothes of a maintenance man, probably from the space-port.

"Hey, A.," said the bartender.

"Hiya," replied the newcomer with a crooked smile. "Not very lively around here."

"Just as dead as ever."

"How about a drink?" He sat down next to Oscar with a sigh.

"Hello, name's Oscar, how about you?" Oscar inquired.

"Oh, hello, didn't notice you for a second. Everybody calls me A." He pulled out a card and handed it to Oscar as he started on his beer.

Oscar read the card:

ANEBULA AWAR-DWINNER
CERTIFIED MECHANIC

Oh, wow. Probably one of his greater achievements in life. I bet he spent half his salary on these cards, Oscar thought.

He handed the card back to Anebula. "Nice name," he remarked.

"Keep it. Buy you a drink?"

"Sure."

"Bartender, two more."

"You're in luck," the bartender pointed out. "It's still happy hour: two for one."

"Work at the spaceport?" Oscar asked A.

"Not now, but I used to be an orbit technician."

Oscar nearly gagged on his free beer. "Get outta town! You wouldn't be in this pit if you had as much money as those guys do!"

"It's true. Let me tell you what happened. First, you know what an orbiting observer is?"

"Yeah, one of those computer complexes built to study a planet, right?"

"Right, and it's as big as a small moon, too. It orbits around the new planet for about five years, gathering information all by itself. But it needs a technical maintenance man. That was my job. You're all alone on the orbiter for five years at a stretch—that's why it pays so well. It can get really scary out there because the place is like one huge echo chamber. You can hear anything that goes on almost anywhere in the entire station. When you go to sleep, that shuffling noise you hear may be your clothes slipping off the dresser, or something else anywhere in the whole orbiter.

"Anyway, I had taken over for this guy who went AWOL, just disappeared. It's not that uncommon, really. So it was now my job. I didn't really mind; in fact, I was ecstatic.

"Well, the first few days were fine, no major malfunctions. But on the fourth day the weirdest thing happened. I was out repairing an electrical connection that had shorted out, when I heard something. It was a slight metallic scraping sound, coming in an irregular pattern. I couldn't figure out what it was. The sound was repeated four times. Then I heard something else. It was like somebody had dropped something that rolled a couple of feet and then was picked up again. And there I was, all alone in that huge, cavernous sphere. No weapons, no nothing."

He paused for a second as if he didn't want to go on. His face was pensive and he seemed very distant and somehow sad. He hesitated again, looked deep into Oscar's eyes, then continued.

"You've never known loneliness until you've been in one of those things. All alone in this huge station where even radio contact takes a month due to Absolute Distance Delay. All you've got is yourself and a big hunk of metal and electronics. It can either be really great—no one is interfering with your life, alone with your thoughts, time for yourself—or it can be really scary . . . all alone.

"For me it was the latter," he said with a laugh.

"Well, I had no idea what the sounds were, but I convinced myself there must be some logical explanation I just couldn't think of. I repaired the connection and started to put the metal panel back over the wiring. When I picked up the screws for the panel, I suddenly realized what the noise had been. Just to make sure, I dropped the screw, let it roll a few inches, and picked it up again.

"That's when I realized that whatever had made the noise could hear me, too. For a few seconds there was silence. It was broken by the gawdawfullest scream I ever heard in my life. It wasn't even human. And then there were footsteps pounding quickly, toward me or away from me, I couldn't tell. So I got on my Moonskipper and skipped away."

Oscar burst out laughing despite the seriousness of the other man's face.

"What in the world is a Moonskipper?"

"That's the only transportation I had on the orbiter," he said with an embarrassed grin. "It's a small ship that travels just above the surface of the station. It's called a skipper because it's made to skip over obstacles. That's what you use to get to the places you have to repair. Every half mile or so there's a thing sticking out of the orbiter that looks like an elevator. It is, actually, except it moves sideways, too. The Moonskipper lands on the one closest to the damaged area, fills the elevator with oxygen, and then you get in. You punch in the coordinates of the area that needs repairing and the elevator takes you there. You strap on your oxygen tank, get out, and make the repair."

"Oh," Oscar replied. He hadn't really followed the explanation. He was more interested in the man.

Anebula's body reflected what he was saying, and his voice fit the mood of the story perfectly. He was living every word of it right there at the bar.

"Well," he said after a pause, "I went back to the base and continued working. There wasn't any way I could find this thing, and the chances of my meeting up with it were astronomically low. Besides, I didn't have much of a choice. But then I realized the thing could call me back, in a way, by damaging something I would have to repair. Even though there were metal panels covering all the wires, they would be no problem for him. So I made my own weapon. I got this laser torch and magnified the power so it could kill. Now I was feeling a little better.

"Thinking back on it, I must have looked pretty silly sneaking around with a laser torch, jumping at every sound, and there were plenty of them! That thing kept making these weird noises. I think it actually meant to scare me. And it wasn't making these sounds with its mouth. It was pounding the walls with something metallic in a rhythmic pattern, like the stalking song of a tronkiil. I was shaking like a shiver rat."

It sounded to Oscar like Anebula had gone insane on the orbiter. He could see how it might drive anyone mad, being alone that long. All the sounds could be explained; the scream could have been the screech of metal, the rhythmic clanking some malfunction of a radar dish accidentally striking something on each rotation. The question was whether Anebula still thought those sounds were made by something alien.

"Then a really major breakdown occurred. A whole section of wiring short-circuited that could take a whole day to repair. So I flew over to the spot and got in the elevator. When I got to the level of repair and the elevator door opened, it was totally dark. Lights were supposed to go on as soon as the door opened, but they didn't. So I had to use a flashlight. I propped the light up to shine on the damage, and then I couldn't see down the hallway. And I heard giggling while I was taking off the metal panel. Every few seconds I'd turn the flashlight on the hallway and grab my laser torch. My hands were shaking so much I could barely get the panel off. And when I did, there was the former technician, dead, with corroded wires running all through him!"

Boy, thought Oscar, *this guy's really flipping out.* Anebula was shaking and sweating; his face paled and his eyes widened, as if he were looking at the dead technician again that very moment. He had a tic in his cheek that was going like mad. *He looks like he's right back on the orbiter hallucinating again. I hope he doesn't die on me or something.*

"His face was all green, and I could tell his neck had been broken. He was partially decomposed. By now the giggling I had heard was a laugh, and though you couldn't tell how close it was, it seemed incredibly near.

"I reached for my laser torch and found nothing: it was gone. I took the flashlight and looked behind me. There stood a creature about seven feet tall, with an ape's mouth, a skull that looked like it contained two brains, and a long, thin body with huge hands and feet. It grabbed me by the throat and brought me close to its face. Then, with a small grin, it squeezed its hand and broke my neck. Life drained from me, and I was a limp doll. Then it stowed me away, like all the others, in some dark corridor of that dreaded moon."

Oscar didn't feel like laughing, but he did. "So you're dead and packed away on the orbiter, are you?"

"Of course."

"Then what are you doing here?"

"Everybody's dead here. This is where everyone comes when they die." He paused, then added, "Now let's hear your story."

"Sorry, boys," the bartender interrupted, "but happy hour is over."

ABOUT THE AUTHOR

Kerry Mitchell lives in Ellettsville, Indiana, where he attends Edgewood High School. He likes reading, playing tennis, writing, and games involving role-playing.

Were his dreams too big to come true?

Prophets

by BRENNAN STASIEWICZ

"Y*ou can always follow a line, but only those who open their eyes can tie it in a knot.*"

Those decaying words, wafting from my grandfather's mouth like dust through sunlight, meant nothing to me. I had lost all interest in listening to the old oracle speak the ways of life. My mind was filled with the more important thoughts of a child: the ever-lasting questions, such as the size of Frankie Perbleman's giant horny toad, and the length of Grandpa's nose hairs. These were the only things encircling my brain, like one of those comic strip word balloons.

The thing that stuck most in my head, however, was about my friend Jim Charlton. Jim and I had been friends ever since we were pea high. Jim was a tall fellow, but not too overpowering. He kept a low profile, but his outside appearance left a long shadow. We often spent long summer nights, lying beneath the stars above the old schoolhouse, talking all deep and serious like we were two prophets from the Bible. It was there, during these nightlong chats, that I really began to see inside Jim. Through these timeless moments of truth it became apparent to me that Jim's seemingly weak outside appearance was only skin deep. If you could look inside Jim as I had, if you could have heard those bronzed words coming from his tight-lipped mouth, you'd be able to see the real Jim. The Jim who could steam his heart past any obstacle. The Jim who emptied his soul to me in sworn secrecy, above the schoolhouse shingles, beneath the innocent stars.

It was two days earlier that Jim had told me of his venture. I played along with him in this game, but, to my discredit, I didn't really believe him. I mean, who in their right mind would ever believe that anyone could do what he was planning?

"Oh, go stick it in the mud," I said as I turned away in disbelief.

"No, Pud." Pud was the natural-sounding nickname that Jim had generously given me. "I swear it on the Bible—ain't nothin' gonna stop me from it."

Still refusing to turn and face him, I spoke from the side of my mouth, "Yeah, like I ain't never heard that from you before!" But then I realized that I never had heard Jim swear to something without doing it. Discreetly, I glanced back at him.

"Aww! Pud! You know I ain't never lied about something like this, and to the contrary, I'm quite insulted!"

I could always tell when Jim was really upset because he'd try to talk like Mrs. Buecher, our English teacher, by using big, highfalutin words and phrases.

"I'm sorry, Jim," I said, now that I saw the flaw in my thinking. "I didn't mean to insult you."

"Yeah, well, now you got me all flabbergasted!"

I looked back down to the ground, found the spot that I had been watching earlier, and forcefully cried, "Shucks! I just think you oughta think about it some more, that's all."

"Well, don't you worry 'bout it, Pud. Now you know that I ain't kiddin'. Just don't tell no one!"

"Why?" I whined with a rolling frown.

"Just don't. I'll be the one who'll tell the town, and I'll do it on . . ." Jim stopped for a moment of thought, "Independence Day. Ju–lie the Fourth!"

The days passed by like a slug through warm beer. I had promised Jim that I would not mention his surprise to anyone, but the suspense and anticipation ate through me. It was Wednesday, two days before the Fourth of July. Mama let me sleep late because we were up till 1:00, playing a wild game of Scrabble. By the time I had dressed, cleaned, and eaten, it was a little past ten. As I looked out the window, I could just feel the thick heat float by the willow tree, to the front porch, and finally take rest over the overgrown bluegrass. I sat down on the old leather recliner in the den and enjoyed the climate. We were one of the first families in town to get an air conditioner. It was able to cool almost every room, but the one that it worked best on was the den. As I sat daydreaming about the beach and cool mountaintops, I sure wasn't looking forward to the chores that were in store for me that day.

I dozed off for a second, but my flights through the Alps soon stopped when Mama entered my cooling cocoon. Before I could say a word, before Mama could say a word, I had the daily list in my face, extracting me from my state of repose. I rose from my cool throne and headed for the reality of an early July day. I stepped out the door and off the front porch, right through that stream of thick, pea soup heat, and took immediate shelter under the willow tree. Hot July mornings are probably the worst times of the year. Not only do you have the sun leeching energy from your helpless body, but you practically have to paddle through the moist air. I stepped around the gardening my mom had set forth for me to do, and decided to visit Jimmy at the malt shop in the middle of town.

I lived in a small Midwestern town called Fleamont. It was probably one of the quietest and dullest towns there had ever been in Oklahoma. Everyone knew everyone, mostly because the population never had exceeded two hundred. Nothing new ever happened except when someone died. There was nothing special about the town, nothing extraordinary, except maybe Mt. Flea. Mt. Flea was not a mountain, but rather a mound. The town took pride in this four-hundred-foot mound because out on the Midwestern plains, there aren't that many geographical formations.

I opened the door to Bubba's Malt and Fine Ice Cream Shop and stepped in. Bubba, after visiting our place last summer, decided to invest in an air conditioner, too. As the dry, arctic air hit me, the change in temperature made my skin feel like it was going to crack. I staggered to the counter and practically passed out onto one of the red vinyl stools. Jim came up and asked like a polite malt boy if he could get me anything. But as soon as Bubba went in the back of the shop, he made me a free malt.

At first I was surprised by his gesture. "What in Sam Hill are you doing?" 'Sam Hill' was a little something that I picked up from Pa. "If Bubba finds out, he'll fire you in a second!" Bubba might not have graduated from high school, but he was one of the smoothest guys in town. Jack McGraw and Bubba Merris, they were the closest things we had to slick, smooth-talking greasers from the city.

Jim had a cool look on his face. "So let the old fart fire me. I'm quittin' after today anyhow. Seeing as how I'm gonna be a star and everything."

"A star? Why are you thinking 'bout being a star?"

"Well, Pud, the way I see it is that there ain't no second best. You either win, or you lose. And I ain't a loser—losers ain't stars."

This was only the second time I'd heard Jim talk like this, the first being five days earlier when he told me his plan. It wasn't like him to be so grown-up about something. He always approached things in a serious manner, but this time it seemed like he wasn't just a kid with a plan, but rather an adult. I wasn't sure how to react to this new Jim, and it seemed that I never would know how to.

One thing was for sure, though. Jim's inflating head was just ballooning out all over the place. Overwhelmed by this transformation in my friend, I just sat back and watched him grow. Besides, if Jim could pull this stunt off, all of Oklahoma would use his name as a household word.

The crowd was growing around the town square

podium like bees around a hive, as all of Fleamont turned out for the Independence Day food and festivities. Jim had put his homemade billboard with the flashy lines, "The once-in-a-lifetime extravaganza affair," over the podium earlier in the day, but hadn't been seen since then. The sign caught the eye of a few townspeople, who, in turn, spread the word to the others who were unaware. So, by about ten in the morning, most of Fleamont was waiting for his surprise.

Finally, at about 10:30, Jim came strutting down Main Street. He had this proud look in his eye, the kind of look the Cannonball Man had when the circus paraded through town. He was almost dressed like him, too. Jim wore painted red boots, green plaid slacks, a magenta shirt, and a black engineer's cap. I figured that he was just doing that to gain attention, and boy, was it working! Jim rose to the platform, waited through a few muffled laughs, and then began to speak.

"For the citizens of Fleamont . . . I, Jim Charlton, will perform one of the most perplexing feats known to man. In fifteen minutes I will approach Mt. Flea, and before the dawn of tomorrow, I will have dug my way to the east side, being armed with nothing but a pick, a shovel, and my determination."

There was a moment of silence, which was met by a roaring laughter that spread like smallpox through the crowd. Jim stood there in silence, still with that self-assured, proud face, a face that reassured me that he would not back down from his plans.

"Go ahead and laugh," Jim said with a little smirk, "but I am going to do what I have said. Believe me or not—it will happen!"

So, with that, Jim jumped from the platform and made his way to the small mountain. I was right behind, following the same path as he, but instead of a pick and shovel in my hand, I had a corndog and ice cream.

Jim had been working now for about four hours. A crowd had gathered around him like at one of those big press conferences, but now he had dug too far into the mass of Mt. Flea for the mob to follow. Picnic blankets and lawn chairs started to fill the area around the east and west side of Mt. Flea.

Gradually, all the festivities of the Fourth of July moved to the mountain. I was having a grand ol' time, but I felt somewhat bad for Jim. He had been working nonstop for ten hours, and by the looks of the black void, he had gone quite a distance. The fireworks took flight over the small pond and winked back at me. Everyone was happy, even Ethel Herfthon, the oldest widow in town. The only one who I could imagine wasn't, was Jim.

At about 10:00 that night, I entered the Jim-made cave with my kerosene lantern, and followed it until I reached him. There he was, working harder than a locomotive. The flashy threads that once reeked of splendor now reeked of intense physical labor. The sweat that rolled from his brow left dark stains on his magenta shirt. His face showed exhaustion and pain, and as I stared at him in awe, I noticed a hot stream of tears flowing from his eyes. I couldn't move or speak for a few minutes. The only thing I heard in the dark cave, besides the grumble of pick and shovel, was Jim's

feeble voice saying, "I ain't stoppin'," over and over
again. I'd never seen anyone work themselves to the
point of crying, not even those guys on the chain gangs
who work on the railroad. I know I will never forget
his face and the way he was at that time for as long as
I live.

"Hey, Jim. Come on, buddy. Let me give you a
hand. Ain't no one gonna find out; everyone's all liquored
up anyhow. Don't do this to yourself."

I offered a few times to help him, just for a little
while, but he refused to have anyone do his work. So,
slowly, I started back out of the tunnel.

The next few hours I sat alone at the base of Mt.
Flea beneath an old, decrepit-looking oak tree. I
didn't talk or mingle with those who remained awake,
drinking and throwing firecrackers at each other. Those
who could not stay awake had drifted home in a tired
and drunken stupor. For the most part, everyone had
lost interest in Jim, and his promise to the town. Even
so, I still believed in him. I believed that he could do
anything he set his mind to, but by doing so, I also believed that he missed those times that form the sweet
memories of childhood. Such memories as that strange
July Fourth, and even memories like Stewy Chipowski's
eighth birthday party. Everyone was at that little bash,
everyone except Jim, who missed it because he was
trying to beat the record for the most crawdads caught
in one day. He was always consumed by one thing after another; unfortunately for him, one thing after another consumed him.

It was about 6:30, and the sun began to awaken

from its bed of clouds over the horizon. The morning dew swept down the generous slopes of Mt. Flea and blew a cool kiss to my cheek. There wasn't any thick heat pouring from the sky, no rain or thunder, just the sound of pick and shovel. I jumped to my feet as my heart began to beat uncontrollably; the first rays of disappointment had not yet broken out of their cover. The wall of dirt and rock started to crumble along the most eastward side of the mountain—Jim was almost here!

Out of the depths of the mound, with one final blow of steel against stone, he came. His weak body turned toward me and gained an inch of posture as he smiled in pitiful appeasement. Then he dropped to the ground in exhaustion and remained there, motionless. In that split second, the mad beat of my heart stopped. I felt my back slide down the smooth, rain-beaten trunk of the oak and come to rest on the cool earth. I lay there for a couple of minutes under the oak, and wept. I cried for many different reasons that day, but most of all for Jim: earlier that morning of July fifth, the sun had risen.

It wasn't until the eighth of July that Jim received what he had worked so hard for. At around 1:00, a man from the *Tulsa Tribunal* stopped by Jim's house for an interview. I sat out on the porch listening to Jim recall everything, from his motives to the satisfaction gained from his—as the reporter put it—"battle against the odds." Most of what I heard Jim tell the reporter wasn't true, but this time I accepted his lies. By Thursday morning, most of Oklahoma had heard of "Jim Charlton's Feat Against the Odds," and Jim finally did become a star.

The fame and glory lasted a few weeks, with some parties and pies, but then it was over. Mt. Flea was the last time I ever saw Jim try to overcome his weaknesses. Mt. Flea was the first time he failed, and I guess this is what changed him. Over the next few years of high school, we both were a little more grown-up from that experience, but most noticeably, Jim.

ABOUT THE AUTHOR

Brennan Stasiewicz wrote this story while a student at Watkins Mill High School in his hometown of Gaithersburg, Maryland. An avid writer, he is also interested in photography and music—"a wide range, from Jimi Hendrix to Bach and Wagner." Snowboarding, baseball, and football are other favorite pastimes.

Story Index
By genre, topic, and for use as writing models

Friendship
The Boy and the Elephant, 57
Song of Masefield, 91
Prophets, 129

The Hero
The Leprechaun's Gold, 23
Quest for Truth, 85
Billy the Seed, 105
Prophets, 129

Nature
The Attack, 81
Quest for Truth, 85
Billy the Seed, 105
Greedy Grant, 113

As Writing Models, cont.
Plot
The Leprechaun's Gold, 23
The Boy and the Elephant, 57
Déjà Vu, 119
Unhappy Hour, 121

Voice
Harry's Hurried Childhood, 11
Dog Days, 29
Goldilocks vs. the Three Bears, 35
In Defense of Hades, 47
Theron, 75
It Ain't Over Till the Fat Lady
   Flings, 115

As Writing Models
Character Development
The Black Stag, 69
Song of Masefield, 91
Billy the Seed, 105
Prophets, 129

Description and Setting
The Curse of Savoll, 37
Quest for Truth, 85
The Story of the Aurora
  Borealis, 97
Greedy Grant, 113

Dialogue
A Modern-Day Fairy Tale, 19
Another Missing Assignment, 67
The Attack, 81
Unhappy Hour, 121

More Fiction By Teen Authors

Merlyn's Pen: The National Magazines of Student Writing

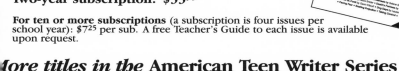

Senior Edition for readers/writers in grades 9-12
Middle School Edition for grades 6-9

Published four times during the school year, *Merlyn's Pen* offers some of the best fiction, essays, and poetry by teen authors.

One-year subscription: $21⁰⁰
Two-year subscription: $33⁹⁵

For ten or more subscriptions (a subscription is four issues per school year): $7²⁵ per sub. A free Teacher's Guide to each issue is available upon request.

More titles in the American Teen Writer Series
New titles every season . . . Teacher's Guides to each title.

Getting There ISBN 1-886427-04-6
Seventh Grade Writers on Life, School, and the Universe
144 pages. $9.⁷⁵* (code GT201A) or $7.²⁵ each for 10 or more (code GT201B). Teacher's Guide: $2.⁹⁵ (code GTGIDE).

Juniors ISBN 1-886427-07-0
Fourteen Short Stories by Eleventh Grade Writers
144 pages. $9.⁷⁵* (code JR201A) or $7.²⁵ each for 10 or more (code JR201B). Teacher's Guide: $2.⁹⁵ (code JRGIDE).

Outsiders and Others ISBN 1-886427-05-4
Stories of Outcasts, Rebels, and Seekers by American Teen Writers
144 pages. $9.⁷⁵* (code OO201A) or $7.²⁵ each for 10 or more (code OO201B). Teacher's Guide: $2.⁹⁵ (code OOGIDE).

Short Takes ISBN 1-886427-00-3
Brief Personal Narratives and Other Works by American Teen Writers
128 pages. $9.⁷⁵* (code TK201A) or $7.²⁵ each for 10 or more (code TK201B). Teacher's Guide: $2.⁹⁵ (code TKGIDE).

Something like a Hero ISBN 1-886427-03-8
Stories of Daring and Decision by American Teen Writers
144 pages. $9.⁷⁵* (code HR201A) or $7.²⁵ each for 10 or more (code HR201B). Teacher's Guide: $2.⁹⁵ (code HRGIDE).

Taking Off ISBN 1-886427-02-X
Coming of Age Stories by American Teen Writers
144 pages. $9.⁷⁵* (code FF201A) or $7.²⁵ each for 10 or more (code FF201B). Teacher's Guide: $2.⁹⁵ (code FFGIDE).

White Knuckles ISBN 1-886427-01-1
Thrillers and Other Stories by American Teen Writers
144 pages. $9.⁷⁵* (code KN201A) or $7.²⁵ each for 10 or more (code KN201B). Teacher's Guide: $2.⁹⁵ (code KNGIDE).

*ADD $2.00 EACH FOR SHIPPING, OR FOR TEN OR MORE COPIES ADD 50¢ EACH.

To order subscriptions and books, call 1-800-247-2027.
Or send check, purchase order, or MC/Visa number (with expiration date and full name) to:

Merlyn's Pen, Dept. ATW
P.O. Box 1058, East Greenwich, RI 02818-0964